ACCEPTING THE DARKNESS

A TALE OF LOVE, LOSS AND ACCEPTANCE

SYED ZIKRA BUKHARI

Made with ♥ on the Notion Press Platform
www.notionpress.com

To my father, who carried the weight of the world on his shoulders so I could walk freely towards my dreams. Your life is a testament to resilience, patience, and unshakable love. You made the impossible seem achievable, even when the odds were against you. "A father's strength is not just in his hands but in his unwavering support, silent sacrifices, and the dreams he builds for his children." .Baba, this book is my humble gift to you—a small reflection of the countless gifts you've given me.

Contents

Acknowledgements

This journey of writing *ACCEPTING THE DARKNESS* would not have been possible without the invaluable people who stood by me at every step.

First and foremost, my deepest gratitude goes to *my father, Syed Shah Hussain Bukhari*. He has always supported me, no matter the circumstance. Having endured so much in his own childhood, he became my first source of inspiration, motivating the very essence of this book.

To *my mother*, a woman of incredible strength, who has also faced hardships for us. She constantly reminds me of who I am and where I belong. "Her arms hold the universe, her heart beats with endless love, and her sacrifices light the path we walk.",

A special thank you to *my teacher, Ruhail Nabi*, the person who gave me direction and made me realize my potential. His wisdom and guidance have been a driving force throughout my journey.

A heartfelt thanka to my uncle" Syed fazil Hussain Bukhari" and" Syed shouib Bukhari", Whose love, guidance and inspiration have shaped my journey.

I extend my gratitude to all my *friends and relatives* whose support, directly or indirectly, gave me the courage to complete this book. Your belief in me means more than words can express.

Lastly, I thank you, *my readers*, for embarking on this journey with me. Your time and attention are gifts I deeply appreciate.

I hope that through the story of Nile, you find reflections of your own life and strength to embrace your own darkness.

Prologue

In the quaint corners of a small town, where laughter dances in the air and dreams take root in the hearts of its inhabitants, there exists a shadow—a darkness that often goes unnoticed. It is the kind of darkness that hides behind smiles, lurking in the depths of unspoken words and unfulfilled dreams. For Nile, a boy shaped by his circumstances, this darkness has become an inseparable companion.

Growing up in a modest home, Nile's life has been marked by hardship and struggle. Poverty is a familiar specter, hovering over him like a cloud, but it is not the only battle he faces. Within the confines of his heart lies a storm of emotions, a tumultuous sea of longing, confusion, and hope. He yearns for connection, for understanding, yet feels trapped in a world where vulnerability is seen as weakness.

It is during this tumultuous journey that he meets Lucy—a girl with a smile that could light up the darkest of nights. Their bond ignites something within him, a flicker of hope amidst the shadows. Yet, as Nile navigates the complexities of friendship and unrequited love, he is forced to confront the deeper truths about himself and the world around him.

But it is not until he meets Lily, a gentle spirit with a heart full of compassion, that Nile begins to truly understand the importance of acceptance. In the dance of their lives, he discovers that darkness does not define him; it is merely a part of the intricate tapestry of existence.

ACCEPTING THE DARKNESS is a journey through the trials of youth, a poignant exploration of love, friendship, and the courage to face one's fears. It is a reminder that within every shadow, there lies the potential for light. And as Nile learns to embrace his darkness, he unveils the beauty that can be found in the struggle.

Join him as he takes the first steps toward understanding that even in the depths of despair, there is a flicker of hope waiting to be discovered.

About The Author

Hello, dear readers! I am *Syed Zikra Bukhari*, a passionate young writer from the enchanting valleys of Kashmir, where every sunset paints a story and every whisper of the wind carries a secret..

After two years of heartfelt dedication, I proudly completed

ACCEPTING THE DARKNESS on 13 September 2024. This book is not merely a collection of words; it is a reflection of my journey—a journey filled with dreams, fears, and the universal struggles that connect us all. Through writing, I've discovered the power of storytelling to heal, inspire, and unite.

Living amidst the breath-taking beauty of Kashmir has profondly shaped my perspective on life and love. Every word in this book is infused with my thoughts, emotions, and the essence of my experiences. I aspire to encourage you, dear readers, to embrace your own journey, find strength in vulnerability, and remember that even in the darkest moments, light is always within reach.

"I wear my scars like armor, fueled by unshaken passion, relentless strength, and sacrifices only the storms of life could demand."

Thank you for joining me on this adventure. Together, let's step into the world of Nile Tyler and discover the beauty that lies within our struggles.

Review

To syed Zikra Bukhari, a rising literary star from Kashmir,

Your novel, Accepting the darkness, is a profound reflection of your immense creativity, emotional insight, and storytelling talent. To craft such a deeply moving narrative at your age is nothing short of extraordinary. Nile's journey, filled with struggle, resilience, and self-discovery, speaks to universal truths, yet you've rendered it personal and poignant, showcasing your remarkable skill in character building and thematic depth.-

Your vivid symbolism---the forest as refuge, the shop as resilience----reveals a maturity beyond your exploration of love, loss, and hope captures the essence of the human spirit. What's even more inspiring is how your writing reflects the beauty and challenges of life in Kashmir, bringing both its struggles and its grace to the forefront.

At just 14, you have already displayed a rare ability to inspire, heal and connect through words. Your courage to explore complex emotions with honesty and empathy is a gift to literature. This novel is a shining star to what promises to be remarkable journey as a writer. Keeping embracing your unique voice ----- your stories have the power to change lives.

With deep admiration,
Dr F.Lone

"Accepting the Darkness" by Zikra Bukhari is a thought provoking novel. The plot framed captivates the reader all through. The writer at this tender age has expressed her emotions and represents the facets of life faced by youth . she artistically dedicates each chapter to a new challenge that the protagonist of her novel goes through and how he discovers his way and strength in the deepest despondent phases of his life.

To this novel is a must addition to the English genre of novel that is beyond romanticism and suspense thrillers. It simply represents life and teaches how to navigate the highs and lows of it with courage. It reminds me of the Quranic Verse that states that we shall be tested with the loss and glad tidings to those who are patient.

Dr.Zaira Ashraf Khan

Assistant Professor, Department of Islamic Studies

GDC Shopian

"I extend my heartfelt appreciation to Zikra for achieving such an indefinable feat. Demonstrating such imagination and depth at such a young age speaks volumes about this bud ding author. The plot, characters, and settings resonate deeply, symbolizing much more than their apparent appearances. The themes and ideas woven into the narrative are universal, seamlessly permeating the life of the protagonist"

"Dear Readers,

Zikra's work is a testament to the power of imagination and storytelling. As you delve into the plot, immerse yourself in the richly crafted characters and the profound themes that transcend the surface.

This story is not just a narrative it is an exploration of universal truths and human emotions. Let it inspire, provoke thought, and leave a lasting impression on your hearts. Happy reading!"

Prof. Mohammad Ishaq

1. Personal and Emotional Connection: The acknowledgment section effectively conveys the authors gratitude and establishes a personal connection with the readers.
2. Vivid Imagery: The introduction to the book and the author's background creates vivid imagery, drawing the reader in to the world of Kashmir.

3. Relatable themes: The story touches on universal themes like self-discovery, resilience and the power of love, making it relatable to readers.

4. Engaging dialogue: The conversation between Nile and Kevin is natural and engaging, allowing the reader to become invested in the story.

Overall, the script shows promise with a strong emotional connection and relatable themes. With revisions to address the weaknesses and suggestions, the story can become even more engaging and immersive for readers.

Regards
Khan Tamjeed

Introduction

In a world where shadows often seem to overpower the light,

ACCEPTING THE DARKNESS invites you to embark on a journey of self-discovery, resilience, and the transformative power of love and friendship.

At the heart of this story is Nile Tyler, a young boy grappling with the complexities of life, navigating the challenges of poverty, friendship, and unspoken emotions. As he faces the darkness that looms around him, he learns that every struggle carries the potential for growth and understanding.

Through the significant moments and relationships in Nile's life—his bond with Lucy, the friendship with Lily, and the profound impact of family—this narrative explores the essence of what it means to be human. It is a tale woven with heart and honesty, reflecting the dreams and aspirations we all hold dear.

Join me in uncovering the journey of Nile as he learns to embrace his darkness, seeking light in the most unexpected places. *ACCEPTING THE DARKNESS* is more than just a story; it is a mirror reflecting our own battles and the hope that resides within us all.

Let's turn the pages together and explore the beauty and complexity of life!

CHAPTER ONE

"One's words are not forgotten, but words have to be forgotten."

It was a day of celebration. Everyone was dressed in their finest clothes, the hall was decorated beautifully, and laughter filled the air. Yet, I found myself sitting alone in a corner, trying to put on my shoes while my thoughts drifted to darker places. I couldn't help but wonder: Where did poverty lead me? I longed for my family to be as wealthy as those around us. The tears I fought so hard to hide from view began to flow freely.

"What's wrong, Nile?" a familiar voice interrupted my thoughts. I looked up to see my friend Lucy standing there, concern etched on her face. I quickly wiped my tears, but Lucy had already noticed.

"Are you crying?" she asked softly.

"No, it's nothing," I replied, trying to sound convincing. "Just something flashed in my eyes." But my uncle's voice cut through the moment.

"How many times have I told you to help in the kitchen? Why are you here?" he barked. I swallowed my hurt and walked away without saying a word, not wanting Lucy to see me in such a vulnerable state.

As I made my way to the kitchen, I glanced back, hoping to apologize to Lucy as I left her alone there. But she had already disappeared. At school the next day, my thoughts were consumed by how to explain my behavior to her. I was deep in thought when suddenly, I was shoved from behind. I stumbled and fell, only to find my classmate Rohan towering over me, accusing me of stealing his money.

"I didn't steal anything!" I pleaded, but he didn't listen. His fists came down hard, and I could do nothing but flee. Exhausted, I ran into a nearby forest. I drank water from a well, ate some fruit from a tree, and found solace under its shade. As I stared up at the canopy, a sense of overwhelming sadness washed over me.

"Oh God, all the colors have been taken from my life," I lamented. "Why me? Why me?" My voice echoed in the silence of the forest. I felt as though I was engulfed by the darkness, a stark contrast to the vibrancy I once knew. I spent the day sleeping there, and when I woke, I made my way home, skipping school.

The next day, I saw Rohan far from me as he was waiting for me, and I ran back to the forest. Days turned into weeks, and I found comfort in the forest's beauty—the vibrant flowers, the sweet scent, and the gentle songs of birds. It became my sanctuary, a place where my colors were restored, and I felt reborn.

Hey! It's me Nile it was the little journey of my life.

My life outside this haven remained a struggle. I had always been different, dressed in torn clothes and carrying worn books, a stark contrast to the other children's polished appearances. My parents, overwhelmed by the burden of a large family, and they sent me to live with my maternal uncle, who treated me like a servant. At school, I was mocked and ridiculed, branded as "ugly" and "black" because of my appearance.

On the first day of school, I was greeted by laughter and insults that felt like daggers. The other students refused to share benches with me, declaring that my presence would dirty them. So, I was left to sit alone at the back of the classroom, surrounded by a sea of empty seats and unkind whispers. Just as I was resigning myself to a day of solitude, a girl with a sweet ponytail, warm brown eyes, and a gentle demeanor approached me.

"Hey! Good morning," she said, extending her hand towards me with a bright smile.

I was taken aback by her unexpected kindness. "Hey, I'm Nile Tyler," I stammered, feeling a flicker of warmth in the cold atmosphere. As our hands met in a handshake, I realized that I was stepping into uncharted territory—this was the biggest mistake of my life. Little did I know how much that simple gesture would change everything.

"I'm Lucy Smith," she introduced herself, her smile radiating a rare and comforting light. In that moment, hope blossomed in my heart, and for the first time that day, I felt like I might not have to face the world alone.

Lucy Smith, my first love, entered my life like a gentle breeze on a sweltering day. With her sweet ponytail swaying and her brown eyes sparkling with kindness, she was a ray of sunshine in my otherwise shadowy world. Her smile lit up the classroom, making it feel a little less intimidating. When she extended her hand to me on that fateful first day, it felt like an invitation to something beautiful.

Looking back, I realize that while Lucy brought moments of joy, she also became a source of confusion and heartache. Our bond was a delicate dance, and in the end, I came to understand that she was also my mistake—a lesson learned in the complexities of love and friendship.

But my relief was short-lived. During a test, the teacher's sharp gaze caught me looking at Lucy's paper. "Cheating!" she barked, her voice echoing ominously in the classroom. Despite my desperate protests, she slapped me hard across the face, the sting of her palm burning with humiliation. She confiscated my test, leaving me frozen in shock.

As tears streamed down my face, I felt utterly alone while the other students continued with their work, indifferent to my plight. Lucy was the only one who noticed my distress. She quickly approached me, her expression filled with concern and empathy. "Nile, it's okay," she whispered softly, her eyes filled with understanding. At that moment, I realized that despite the chaos and judgment surrounding me, I had found a connection—a bond that might just help me navigate through the darkness ahead.

At home, I would often smile to mask my pain, but the harsh reality of my situation was ever-present. One day, I asked my mother why she sent me away and why I had to endure such hardship. Her reply was filled with sorrowful wisdom: "I think God has something good in store for us, but we must be patient. Patience is Key. Everything will be alright in time."

I laughed bitterly at her words, feeling broken inside. I felt my mother's pain and understood that her smiling facade hid her own struggles. She placed her hand on my head and said, "I know how much pain you're hiding behind that smile. I have endured the same. But remember, no matter how difficult the journey or destination, always keep smiling and never let the obstacles break you."

Her words were a lesson in resilience. As I faced the trials of my life, I learned to maintain my strength and composure, refusing to be broken by the challenges ahead.

"But what can be done? My misfortune persisted despite the promise I made. Soon after, something terrible happened to me."

CHAPTER TWO

After enduring numerous challenges, I found myself disheartened. However, a conversation with my cousin Kevin was a turning point. His words resonated with me deeply and provided the motivation to persevere. Initially, I worked diligently, but over time, my circumstances caused me to falter. Kevin advised me that if studying was not an option for me, I should do everything in my power to ensure my siblings could continue their education. He urged me to be a source of light for my parents, who were struggling in the dark. "Be a pillar of support for them," he said. "If you become emotional, what will your family do? Study hard."

I confided in Kevin about the teasing I faced at school because of my appearance and my sense of feeling unloved. He responded seriously, "Don't let them get to you. There are three magical words that will transform your life. It's not 'I love you,' but 'what people think.' If you focus on what others think, you'll never succeed. People are like barking dogs; they do it out of habit, not because it matters."

Kevin shared an experience from his coaching sessions where he faced ridicule for having red eyes. Instead of crying, he confidently responded, "It's better than your ugly faces," which silenced his mockers. He advised me not to show weakness, as it would only invite more negativity. "No matter how innocent you are, people will still perceive you as cruel," he said. "So don't be innocent. Behind every good face, there can be a hidden edge." I nodded, understanding his message, and we went downstairs for dinner.

On Monday morning, as I was getting ready for school, I called Kevin.

Me: "Get ready if you're coming to school later."

Kevin: "I wanted to come, but I'm not well. I can't make it." Me: "What's wrong?"

Kevin: "Just a bit of fever and a cough." Me: "You'll be fine soon."

Kevin was my beacon in the storm, a bright and supportive cousin who always seemed to know when I needed him most. His laughter could light up the darkest days, and his unwavering belief in me made all the difference. Whenever I found myself drowning in despair, Kevin would pull me back to the surface with his words of encouragement, reminding me that I was stronger than I thought.

"Hey, Nile," he would say, his voice filled with warmth. "Remem- ber, it's okay to feel lost sometimes. We all have our battles, but you're not fighting them alone." His presence was a comforting shield against the harshness of the world.

He had this remarkable ability to make everything feel manage- able, like no challenge was too great to overcome. "You've got this," he'd insist, a smile spreading across his face. "Just take it one step at a time." Kevin understood the weight I carried and never hesitated to shoulder some of it himself.

As I looked back on our moments together, I realized that he was more than just a cousin—he was my anchor, my confidant, and my friend. In a world filled with uncertainty, Kevin was my constant, a reminder that even in the toughest times, there was always hope and light to be found.

As I stepped into school that day, the excitement in the air was palpable. Our teacher walked in, her smile brighter than usual, and announced, "Class, I have wonderful news! You all have a month-long vacation ahead of you! Enjoy every moment!"

Cheers erupted, filling the classroom with joy. My heart raced at the thought of freedom and adventure. I began packing my bag, imagining all the fun times we would have with friends and family.

Suddenly, Lucy appeared at my side, holding a small, beautifully wrapped box. "Hey, Nile! I have something special for you," she said, her eyes sparkling like stars.

"What's this?" I asked, my curiosity piqued as I reached for the box.

"It's a gift! Just a little something to celebrate the break," she replied, a shy smile gracing her lips.

As I unwrapped the colorful paper, my breath caught at the sight of a delicate bracelet adorned with vibrant beads. "Wow, Lucy! This is amazing! Thank you so much!" I exclaimed, overwhelmed by her thoughtfulness.

"I'm so glad you like it," she said, her cheeks flushed with happiness. "I thought it might bring you good luck this vacation."

"Good luck? With you around, I already feel like the luckiest guy!" I joked, trying to keep the mood light, and she laughed, a sound that made my heart flutter.

"Promise me you'll wear it," she urged, her eyes earnest.

"I promise," I said, slipping the bracelet onto my wrist. "Every time I look at it, I'll think of you!"

With a wave, she dashed off to join her friends, leaving me with a warm glow in my heart. I couldn't stop smiling as I walked home, the bracelet shining brightly as a reminder of our blossoming friendship.

The next two weeks flew by in a whirlwind of laughter, games, and late-night talks. Every moment felt magical, a fleeting dream I wished would never end. But as the days blended together, an ominous cloud began to loom over our happiness.

One fateful night, my father had decided to go somewhere in the car, My father was the brightest star in my universe, the person I admired most. He was everything I aspired to be—kind, strong, and endlessly supportive. Growing up, I adored him more than anyone else. His laughter filled our home with warmth, and his stories were treasures I held onto tightly.

But there was a shadow that followed him, a quiet shame that he carried. He often felt he couldn't provide enough for us, despite his unwavering love and dedication. I could see it in his eyes, the way he would look at us with a mix of pride and guilt, as if he believed he was failing us. I wished he could see the happiness I experienced in small victories, the progress I made in school, and the friendships I forged.

Whenever I came across his picture, a wave of longing washed over me. I wanted him to see the man I was becoming, to witness my journey and understand that I was trying my best. I wanted to tell him that his teachings still guided me through my darkest days, but I also wanted him to know how deeply I loved him.

In those moments, I felt the weight of his absence even more. I wished he could be here, not just to share in my triumphs but to realize that he had given me everything I needed to face the world. I hoped that, somehow, he could sense my struggles and victories, that he could find peace in knowing how much he meant to me, even if he felt ashamed of not doing enough.

And when darkness fell, he still hadn't returned. Worry gnawed at me, but I shrugged it off, convincing myself he was just caught in traffic. I curled up in bed, hoping to see him walk through the door any moment.

Suddenly, a loud knock jolted me awake, sending adrenaline coursing through my veins. I raced to the door, flinging it open to find two police officers standing on the porch, their faces serious and grim.

"What's wrong?" I gasped, dread pooling in my stomach.

"Can we speak with you and your family?" one officer asked, his tone heavy with unspoken sorrow.

My heart raced. "Is everything okay?"

"I'm afraid we have bad news. Your father was in a car accident," he said, each word like a knife piercing my heart. "He didn't survive."

Time seemed to freeze. The world around me blurred as reality crashed down like a tidal wave, dragging me under. "No… no, it can't be true!" I cried, feeling my legs buckle beneath me.

I staggered back, gripping the door frame for support as panic coursed through my veins. Memories of my father flooded my mind—his laughter, his strength, his unwavering love. Tears streamed down my cheeks as the reality settled in, crushing my spirit.

The officers tried to offer their condolences, but their words were muffled, lost in a sea of disbelief. My father, my hero, was gone. I felt as though I were standing on the edge of a precipice, staring into an abyss of despair.

I wanted to scream, to shake this nightmare away, but all I could do was cry, each sob echoing the unbearable loss that now defined my life. My father had always been my guiding light, and now, in the suffocating darkness, I felt utterly lost.

As the weight of my father's absence settled heavily in my chest, a vivid memory flickered to life in my mind—a moment etched in my heart forever. I could see us standing by the old stone well, the sun shining brightly overhead. We were pulling water, the rhythmic sound of the bucket splashing resonating through the stillness of the afternoon. My father had let go of the rope for a moment, his eyes sparkling with mischief as he turned to me.

"Sometimes, Nile," he had said, "situations become difficult. It's easy to feel overwhelmed, like we're pulling against an unyield- ing force. But remember, patience is the key. Sometimes, you just need to let the rope slip and trust that things will get better."

His words were simple yet profound, a lesson I carried with me through every challenge I faced. I remembered how I had nodded earnestly, soaking in his wisdom like the sun's warmth. I had never imagined then how those words would resonate so deeply in a moment like this.

Now, standing in the shadows of my grief, I took a deep breath, trying to gather the strength my father had always shown. I knew my mother was suffering, her face pale and drawn with sorrow. I wrapped my arms around her, pulling her close, feeling the tremors of her grief echoing through me.

"Mom, we need to be strong," I whispered, my voice steadying despite the tears blurring my vision. "Dad always taught us that patience and resilience will guide us through even the darkest times. We're not alone in this. We have each other."

Her sobs quieted slightly as she looked into my eyes, searching for comfort amidst the storm of emotions swirling around us. "But how do we move on without him?" she asked, her voice barely above a whisper.

"We carry him with us," I replied, my heart aching. "We hold onto his lessons, his love, and his spirit. He's still here, in everything we do, in every decision we make. We owe it to him to live fully, to honor his memory."

As I spoke, I felt a flicker of hope igniting within me, pushing against the darkness. I knew it wouldn't be easy, that grief would come in waves, but I also knew that my father's strength was now part of me. I would lean into that strength and allow it to guide us through the pain.

"Together, we can face this," I said, squeezing her hand tightly, drawing strength from the bond we shared. "We will find a way to heal, one day at a time."

And in that moment, I realized that while my father had left this world, his lessons and love would forever be our anchor, guiding us as we navigated the storm of our lives. We would pull together, just as we had at the well, and through patience and resilience, we would find our way back to the light.

Three months had passed since that devastating night, and now I stood on the precipice of a new chapter: returning to school. Each step felt heavy, weighed down by the loss of my father and the dreams I had once cherished. I forced myself to look at my mother, who was valiantly trying to mask her pain behind a brave face. "I'll manage, Mom," I said, attempting to sound more confident than I felt. But inside, I was still grappling with a storm of emotions, clinging to the memory of my father's encouraging words about saving money for emergencies.

Studying had never been my passion; I had always preferred to express myself through painting. Yet, my mother had never truly supported that dream, her focus solely on academics and what she believed would secure a stable future for me

As I readied myself to leave, I caught a glimpse of my mother's pain reflected in her eyes, a mirror of my own heartache. I quickly turned away, fighting back tears that threatened to spill over. "Just keep moving forward," I whispered to myself, recalling my father's comforting presence and the lessons he had imparted.

When I reached my maternal home, I was faced with a dilemma that tugged at my conscience. I had saved a small amount of money—my father's last gift—intended for emergencies. Should I give it to my mother, who was struggling to keep our lives afloat, or should I use it to pursue my own dreams? The weight of that choice pressed heavily on my shoulders.

Just then, my aunt called me for dinner, pulling me from my spiraling thoughts. I took a moment to close my piggy bank, feeling the cold metal of the coins and the warmth of memories associated with them. "What would Dad want me to do?" I wondered, wrestling with the conflicting emotions.

Sitting at the dinner table, surrounded by laughter and chatter, I felt out of place. Everyone seemed to move on while I felt stuck in this whirlwind of grief and uncertainty. I was just in the 10th grade, a time that was supposed to be filled with hope and ambition, yet I felt overwhelmed by the challenges ahead. Would I ever find my way back to that light? Would I be able to paint my dreams onto the canvas of my life again?

In that moment, I realized that I had a choice to make. I could either allow my circumstances to dictate my future or take a stand, channeling my pain into something meaningful. Perhaps my father's words about saving money for emergencies were not just about finances but about preparing me for the battles that lay ahead. I took a deep breath, feeling a spark of determination igniting within me. I was still here, still alive, and maybe, I could find a way to rebuild my dreams, one brushstroke at a time.

CHAPTER THREE

One restless night, I sat by the window, my mind tangled in a web of worries about the future. The absence of my father weighed heavily on me, and I struggled with thoughts of how to care for my family. Just then, a soft knock broke the silence. It was Kevin, my cousin, who walked in quietly and gestured for me to sit down. He sat opposite me, leaning forward with a seriousness I hadn't seen before.

And he spoke up "Listen, Nile. I know things are tough. Your father's gone, and life feels upside down right now, but you need to stay patient. You can't give up—not now. You have to be strong for your family. You're the man of the house now."

His words hit me like a tidal wave, and my eyes welled up with tears.

He stopped me and said "No, no," he said gently, putting his hand on my shoulder. "Not now, Nile. There will be a time to cry, but not tonight. Right now, you have to stand tall. Tell me what's troubling you. I promise—whatever it is, we'll figure it out together."

At first, I hesitated, but something about his sincerity made me open up.

And I said "I don't know what to do, Kevin. My father used to give me money, and I've kept it in a piggy bank all this time. But now… now I don't know what I should do with it. And it's driving me crazy."

Kevin: "How much do you think is inside?" Me: "I don't know exactly. I never counted it."

Kevin: "Then let's open it and see."

I shook my head, clutching the piggy bank close. **"No, Kevin, I can't. This is the last thing my father gave me. It's the only part of him I have left—I don't want to break it."**

Kevin gave me a compassionate smile. "I understand, Nile. But sometimes, holding on too tightly keeps us from moving forward. Let's look inside—just once. I promise, I'll help you take care of it afterward."

Reluctantly, I agreed. We carefully broke open the piggy bank, and out spilled a collection of notes and coins—amounting to about $36. The sight of it made my heart ache, but it also gave me hope.

Kevin spoke up "With this, we can start something. How about a small shop? It may not seem like much now, but it'll grow."

The idea sounded strange at first—starting a business in the midst of so much chaos? But the more Kevin talked, the more it made sense.

The next morning, we set out with a plan. "Our shop wouldn't be fancy—just a simple wooden stall covered with large leaves." The challenge was finding the right location. I suggested setting it up right outside the school. It was a smart idea since students could stop by during their breaks, but the thought of rain ruining our hard work troubled us.

Kevin: came up with a practical solution: "Whenever it looks like rain, we'll pack everything and take it home. It'll be a hassle, but we'll manage." His optimism lifted my spirits.

That same day, we gathered wood, leaves, and a few school friends to help us build the shop. It wasn't much—a simple structure pieced together with whatever materials we could find—but it felt like the start of something meaningful. Every nail we hammered and every leaf we placed gave me a sense of purpose I hadn't felt in a long time.

Once the shop was set, we headed to the market to buy some basic supplies: snacks, cold drinks, stationery, and even set up a small tea stall to attract more customers. Kevin and I divided shifts—he ran the shop in the mornings, and I took over in the afternoons after school. Our little venture quickly became popular among students who dropped by during breaks, and soon, we were making decent profits.

However, managing everything wasn't easy. "Balancing school, homework, and the shop was overwhelming." There were nights I stayed up late finishing assignments and mornings where I struggled to stay awake in class. But giving up wasn't an option. "With every obstacle, I thought of my father's words about patience and persistence."

One evening, as we packed up the shop before the rain hit, I looked over at Kevin. "This is harder than I thought," I admitted, exhausted.

Kevin grinned, patting my shoulder. "Of course it's hard, Nile. But look at what we've built together. Your father would be proud."

Hearing those words gave me the strength to keep going. Our shop wasn't just a way to earn money—it became a symbol of resilience. "Through every challenge, I learned that even when life pushes you to the edge, you can rebuild—one small step at a time."

And so, our little shop stood—not just as a wooden structure covered with leaves, but as a beacon of hope. "A reminder that no matter how broken things feel, you can start again and find a way forward."

"When you start something, don't lose hope," I remember telling myself that every single day when I first opened the shop. It felt like everything was slipping out of my hands. I wasn't sure if I could manage it—handling customers, keeping the shelves stocked, running the place all on my own. Honestly, I felt like giving up so many times. Nothing seemed to go right at first.

But I held on. Step by step, I figured things out. It wasn't easy— some days were harder than others. But here's what I learned: It's okay to stumble in the beginning. It's okay to feel lost. What matters is you keep going. You push through the doubt, through the fear. The beginning of anything will always be the toughest part—but it's also where the magic lies if you don't give up.

Looking back now, I realize how much I've grown from those moments. And no matter what life throws at me, I know one thing for sure—if you believe in what you're doing, you'll find your way.

How could I ever forget Uzair—the one who made that shop feel like it would last forever? Through every struggle, he stood beside me, never letting me fall behind. Whenever things got too hard, he had this way of lightening the mood with a joke or a smile, as if to say, "We've got this."

I still remember the first time I saw Uzair. It was a rainy morning, and the school corridors were buzzing with chatter. I was sitting by myself on a bench near the classroom, trying to blend into the background like always. I didn't have many friends back then—just a kid lost in the crowd, hoping no one would notice him.

That's when 'he' walked in—a new student, just like me once. Uzair entered the classroom with this goofy grin, his uniform slightly wrinkled, and his backpack hanging lazily off one shoulder. He looked… different. Confident but not arrogant. Carefree, like the rain outside didn't bother him one bit. There was this odd energy around him—like life was just a big joke, and he was in on it.

He scanned the room, looking for a place to sit, and for a moment, our eyes met. I quickly looked away, pretending to scribble something in my notebook. I figured he'd walk past me and sit with the cooler kids, like everyone else did. But instead, he plopped down right next to me.

"Hey," he said, flashing a wide grin. "I'm Uzair. New here. You look like you could use a friend."

I didn't know what to say. Nobody had ever approached me like that accept Lucy —so straightforward, so friendly.

He nudged my arm, "Do they make us write essays on the first day? Or is this just your idea of fun?"

I laughed, despite myself, for the first time in what felt like ages. That laugh… it felt like someone cracked open a window in a room I'd been locked in for too long.

From that moment on, Uzair stuck to me like glue. We were complete opposites—he was loud and full of mischief, while I was quiet and cautious—but somehow, it worked. He had this way of dragging me into things I'd never have done on my own—like sneaking out of school during recess to buy snacks from the shop down the street or convincing me to join the football team even though I could barely kick a ball straight.

He didn't just become a friend; he became 'the' friend. The one who stood by me when things got tough. The one who could make me laugh even on the darkest days. And somewhere along the way, without even realizing it, Uzair became my brother. And as our friendship grows I came to know that he was an orphan got scholarship here. He was alone, struggling and surviving.

CHAPTER FOUR

It was a very normal day for me. I lost track of everything and went to the shop. When I got there, I saw Lucy was already sitting inside. I approached her and asked, "Lucy, what are you doing here? You didn't inform me."

"You were talking about your shop at school, so I thought I'd come see it. Did I do something wrong?" she replied.

"No, that's alright. But you mentioned in school that you are going home," I said.

"Hey, we'll discuss these things later. First, show me your shop," she insisted.

After showing her around the shop, we sat down to drink tea. I began to tell Lucy everything about Uzair. As I spoke, I noticed she was looking at me with an air of irritation. When I finished, she said, "So you got a new friend better than me? I really want to be nice to you Nile"

She explained this to me for a long time. I initially thought she was concerned about me, but I realized later that she was merely putting on an act. After our lengthy conversation, she stood up and said, "I think it's getting late. I should go home now." We shook hands, and she left.

Later that evening, I closed the shop and went home

Next day, as I was walking back from school, I spotted Uzair sitting on the side of the road, right by the school gate. At first, I thought he might just be up to one of his usual antics, but as I got closer, I noticed something different—his grin was missing.

"Uzair?" I called, walking towards him. "What are you doing here, man?"

He looked up at me, stretched out lazily on the ground like he didn't have a care in the world. "Tired," he said with a shrug. "Thought I'd rest here for a bit."

I sat down next to him, my bag resting beside me. The air felt heavy, and for some reason, I could tell something was off. Uzair wasn't his usual self—no teasing, no jokes. Just silence. It was weird, like he was lost in thoughts that didn't belong to him.

"You okay?" I asked, nudging him gently. "Something on your mind?"

He let out a deep sigh. "Just… trying to figure things out." He leaned back against the wall. "I got to do some work, Nile. I can't survive here without earning a little, but it's been four days, and I still haven't found anything."

His words hit me differently. This was Uzair—the guy who always made everything sounds like a breeze. Hearing him say this felt strange, and it stuck with me. That's when an idea crossed my mind.

I remembered the shop—the one Kevin and I used to manage but hadn't touched in a while. It had been gathering dust ever since we got too busy with school and other things. We had no time to keep it running, and it seemed like the perfect opportunity.

"Hey…" I said slowly, "the shop—remember it? Kevin and I barely have time for it anymore, and it's mostly closed these days. But if you're up for it… maybe we could bring it back to life? You, me, and Kevin. What do you think?"

Uzair's eyes lit up, that familiar spark returning to his face. "You serious?" he asked, sitting up straight. "You think it'll work?"

I nodded. "Yeah, man. If we team up, it'll definitely work. We can get things running again, and you'll have something to keep you going."

He gave me a wide grin, the Uzair I knew returning in an instant. "Alright then, let's do it," he said with a new excitement in his voice.

And just like that, we made a decision that would change everything. We didn't know it back then, but that shop would become more than just a place for us to work—it would become our escape, our shared dream, and the place where everything in our lives began to unfold.

He was thrilled and hugged me. I then explained when, where, and what time he could work at the shop. He agreed enthusiastically. Later, at school, I suggested we check the shop after classes. He nodded in agreement.

When we arrived at the shop, I was concerned Lucy might react negatively upon seeing Uzair. However, she didn't seem to care. I approached her and whispered, "This is Uzair, the person I told you about yesterday."

She acknowledged with a nod. I was surprised but decided to move on. Uzair wanted to see the shop, so I showed him around. I told him that I usually earned around $3 for two hours of work, but if he worked continuously, we could make up to $4. He agreed.

Lucy suddenly stood up and said, "Can you guys talk about something else, please?" We sat down and began discussing other topics. Despite my attempts to focus, my mind kept drifting. I couldn't shake the thought that Uzair was quite attractive. I wondered what I would do if Uzair liked Lucy or if Lucy had feelings for him. These thoughts seemed strange, but Uzair's eyes remained fixed downward, showing no particular interest in Lucy.

After a while, Lucy announced, "I think I'm late. I'm heading home now." When she left, Uzair and I continued discussing the shop. We parted ways afterward.

His words resonated deeply. As he prepared to leave, I realized that the challenges of life were not as daunting as they seemed. With Kevin's advice echoing in my mind, I faced the uncertain future with renewed.

CHAPTER FIVE

The next morning, as I was getting ready for school, I wandered into Kevin's room. He was sitting on the edge of his bed, wearing a new shirt, a small suitcase lying open beside him. It immediately felt strange—out of place. I leaned against the door frame, forcing a smile. "That doesn't look like a new school uniform," I joked lightly.

He turned to me with a small, sad smile. The kind of smile that feels more like a farewell than a greeting. Something heavy hung in the air, and I knew it wasn't good.

"Are you going somewhere?" I asked, my heart tightening.

"Yeah... My grades are really bad, Nile. I failed miserably in 10th grade. My parents decided I need a fresh start, so they're sending me to London for school," he replied softly.

I blinked, hoping I had misheard. Kevin was more than a friend to me—he was a lifeline, someone who had always stood by me when the world turned cold. "Come on, this has to be a joke, right? Don't mess with me, Kevin."

But he shook his head. "No joke. I'm leaving."

Panic welled up inside me. "You can't just leave! You know what it's like for me. You've seen how people treat me. Without you, it'll be worse. Please, don't go. If you leave, I… I won't even go back home."

Kevin sighed deeply, as though he was carrying the weight of both our troubles. "Nile, you can't depend on me forever. You leaned on your father, and now he's gone. If you keep clinging to others, how will you ever stand on your own? Will you cry forever? Life doesn't stop just because things get hard."

His words pierced through me like cold wind on bare skin.

"You're scared of losing people, but fear isn't a place to live, Nile. You have to face it. When you keep running from fear, it grows like a shadow that follows you everywhere. But shadows are just tricks of the mind—they only exist if you keep looking back. The moment you look forward and keep walking, fear loses its grip on you."

I swallowed the lump in my throat, unable to say anything. His voice softened, though the weight of his words still lingered.

"Life isn't easy—it never will be. But you've got to stop looking back. Don't let what's gone pull you down. You have to move forward, no matter how hard it feels."

For a long moment, we sat in silence, the room thick with unspoken emotions. His words echoed in my mind, filling every corner of my heart.

Kevin reached out, placing a hand on my shoulder. "You've got this, Nile. You're stronger than you know. Just remember—if you keep walking forward, no shadow can touch you."

I nodded slowly, trying to absorb the weight of his words. Though my heart ached, I knew he was right. Kevin was leaving, and I had no choice but to stand on my own.

He gave me one last reassuring smile before picking up his suitcase. That was the kind of friend Kevin was—a guiding light, even in his absence. And as he walked out of the room, I knew his words would stay with me long after he was gone.

For the first time, I promised myself to stop looking back.

When I got home, Kevin was getting ready to leave. Before stepping out, he called me aside for one last conversation. His expression was serious, the kind of look you give someone when you know your words will linger long after you're gone. "Listen, Nile," he began softly, "as I told you this morning, no one will be there when you're drowning in your own storm. People have a way of vanishing when you need them the most, leaving you to fend for yourself. I know Lucy is important to you—maybe even more than you realize—but have you noticed how she disappears the moment things get tough? You think she's standing beside you, but all she's doing is watching from a safe distance, leaving you to sink when the tide gets high."

His words struck deep, but I couldn't deny the truth that flickered inside them. He exhaled slowly and continued, "Nile, a magician creates beautiful illusions—things that seem too good to be false— but in the end, it's all just a trick. I think Lucy is doing the same. She stays close when it's convenient, but when life starts demanding loyalty, she slips away. She'll use you for her needs, and when she's done, she'll leave you behind with some excuse so polished; it'll feel like it's your fault. You'll stand there, trying to piece together what happened, wondering where things went wrong."

He paused, giving me a moment to absorb his words. "I'm not saying you should cut her off. Be polite. Talk to her. But don't bare your soul, Nile. Some people only need to know your secrets once to ruin your life later. Keep your distance—not in the way others see, but where it matters most, in your heart. You think you know her now, but time reveals everything. When that moment comes, I hope you'll remember what I've told you."

I clenched my fists, frustration bubbling beneath the surface. "How can you be so sure?" I asked my voice barely steady. "What makes you think she's not genuine? You can't judge people just by what they show on the surface—maybe there's more to her than you known."

Kevin gave me a soft, knowing smile, the kind that feels more like a farewell than an answer. "That's the thing, Nile—only time can tell you the truth. But when that truth finally catches up to you, I hope it won't be too late to protect yourself."

He stepped closer and pulled me into a tight hug. In that embrace, I felt a strange mix of comfort and sorrow, as if I were holding onto the last moments of something I wasn't ready to let go of. It reminded me of the way my father used to hug me, like he wanted to keep me safe even when life wouldn't.

"Goodbye, Nile," Kevin whispered into my ear, his voice laced with both warmth and finality. "We'll meet again someday, but until then… be careful." And with that, he turned and walked away into the fading light.

A heavy ache settling in my chest. Kevin's words echoed in my mind, each one cutting deeper than the last. His warning wasn't just about Lucy—it was about the world, about trust, about surviving in a place where people could be both companions and illusions.

And as much as I hated to admit it, Kevin was right. Only time would tell who would stay by my side and who would leave me when I needed them the most.

I was deeply upset, though I tried not to show it. As he started to leave, I grabbed his hand and said with some anger, "How do you think she's using me for her own means? What have you seen in her that makes you believe she's not good for me? People can't always be judged by their faces. Their hearts might be different from what they show. So what makes you think she's not sincere?"

He smiled and placed his hand on mine. "Only time will tell you.

I can't explain it to you completely now. When the time comes, it will reveal the mistake you're making. I think it's getting late; we should go." He pulled me into a tight hug. It felt like my father was hugging me, and I didn't want to let go. He said, "We will meet again after a long time. Goodbye and left.

I was a little upset so I made my way to home

As I entered, I was horrified to see that she was very ill with a high fever. My siblings were gathered around her. I asked one of my brothers what had happened, and he explained that she had developed a high fever the previous evening. Papa's friend had come, called a doctor, and they had treated her. Now she was resting while we had played in the kitchen. The electricity had gone out, so we were frightened and slept with Mom.

I went to my mother, took her hand, and said, "You told me to be like ice in every situation and not to melt in front of the sun. But now you're melting. Was the sun too hot?"

In a weak voice, she replied, "Yes, dear son, the sun was too hot, and I melted. I'm sorry I couldn't stay like ice, but you have to remain strong." I showed her the money and told her about the shop. Her eyes lit up with happiness, and she held my hand tightly.

As time passed, I studied often with Kevin. When he wasn't around, I studied with Uzair and Lucy. We got along well.

Eventually, I bought a phone and made my first call to Kevin. We talked for a long time. I realized we always need someone in our lives—a partner, friend, cousin, or parent—with whom we can share our sorrows. It's essential. When I stayed at my maternal home, I felt very lonely. Initially, Kevin was with me, but when he left, I was utterly alone. Whenever my aunt scolded or beat me, I couldn't speak to anyone, not even my family. I would cry in my room and ask the moon, "You always sit alone; don't you fear the darkness?"

In my imagination, the moon seemed to reply, "Oh dear! I have my own life and shine brightly. If I feared the darkness, you wouldn't see me shining in the night sky. If I gave in to fear, I'd disappear, and you would never see me."

This imaginary conversation gave me a lot of courage. Eventually, I upgraded my wooden shop to a proper store. Uzair, Lucy, and I studied and worked there. Although we played a lot, which wasn't ideal for success, I realized that success requires navigating difficult paths. Easy paths don't lead to success. We often seek comfort and avoid facing challenges, but those difficulties are part of life.

I tried to study by the river but would always return to join them. Despite my efforts, breaking this habit was tough. One night, I made a promise to myself to give up this habit. The next day, I went to the river with a book. At first, it was difficult, and my heart urged me to return. But I persevered. Gradually, it became easier, and I found myself enjoying the distance.

As the days passed, I found myself falling deeper for Lucy. Her kindness had a way of wrapping around my heart, like a warm blanket on a cold winter's day. Every smile she shared felt like sunlight breaking through the clouds, illuminating the shadows that had once consumed me.

I began to cherish every moment we spent together, the laughter we shared, and the quiet glances that lingered just a moment too long. Each conversation was a melody that played in my mind long after we parted ways, and I could hardly focus on anything else.

Finally, the day arrived when I felt ready to reveal my feelings. My heart raced at the thought, a mix of excitement and fear swirling within me. Would she feel the same? Would I be brave enough to let her know just how much she meant to me? I took a deep breath, reminding myself that this moment could change everything. As I approached her, I felt the weight of my emotions pressing against my chest, urging me to speak the truth that had been hidden for far too long.

On that day, as I was about to head to the river, I saw Lucy sitting there, looking sad. I approached her and asked, "Hey! Why is the fairy of beauty so sad?" She looked at me and said, "Whether I'm happy or sad is none of your concern. What I want to do is none of your business, and why should I answer you?"

She often joked around, so I thought she was playing with me. I said, "I'm not in the mood for jokes. Tell me what's wrong."

Lucy stood up, and I did too. She said, "Nile, I need to tell you something. We can't be friends anymore. I'm sorry, but we need to stay away from each other. It's better for both of us."

I wasn't surprised or upset. I thought maybe she was just angry and that things would be fine after a few days. I planned to talk to her again later. How naive I was—I understand that now. Resolved compassionate.

CHAPTER SIX

The next day at school, I sat on my bench, staring out the window. To my dismay, I saw Rohan and Lucy walking together, holding hands. I quickly turned my gaze forward to avoid seeing them. When they came into the classroom and sat together, I was taken aback. Until yesterday, I thought Lucy's words had been a joke, but now I began to question if she had been serious.

Uzair arrived and sat next to me. He noticed my distress and asked, "Hey, what's going on? Lucy always sat with you. What's happening?"

I didn't respond and just opened my book, which made Uzair realize that something was wrong. The class teacher came in and started the lesson, but I couldn't focus. My attention was fixed on Rohan and Lucy. As soon as class ended, I approached Lucy and said, "Let's set aside our anger and talk like we used to."

Lucy looked at me with visible irritation. That was when I recognized my mistake—trying to be friends with Lucy. She stood up and began to speak loudly. "Nile Tyler, what do you think of yourself? Are you some big movie star or something special? Everyone, listen up! This is Nile, who wanted to be my friend. He wanted me to do everything he said. Nile, who do you think you are? I've been telling you for two days to stay away from me, but you're still following me around like a dog. I never intended to be friends with you. That day, when you were sitting alone in class like a lonely boy, I reached out just to keep you company. We were never friends and never will be. Keep this in mind—because you haven't seen my worst side yet. I am twice as bad as I am good. So it's best for you to stay away from me. If you come near me again, things will get worse. You've lost all your respect now. Take your bag and go home."

Crying, I picked up my bag and fled the school. I wandered aimlessly, not heading home or anywhere specific. I ended up sitting outside a shop, crying uncontrollably. The shop owner noticed me and came over, asking, "My son, why are you crying like this? Has someone died, or have you been hurt?"

I looked up and said, "Oh uncle, I wish someone had died. That would be easier than this pain," and I walked away.

From that day on, Lucy treated me poorly. Her actions were intended to bring me down, and to some extent, they did affect me deeply. I cried a lot, but from that sadness, I grew stronger and more resilient. Lucy's treatment led me to start misbehaving with everyone. I isolated myself and began arguing with Uzair over trivial matters.

One day, while Uzair and I were working at the shop, I suddenly stood up and went to the river, sitting there in solitude. Uzair followed and placed a comforting hand on my shoulder. "What's happened to you, Nile? You've changed so much. Why are you like this now?"

I snapped back, "Yes, I've changed. Do you have a problem with that? Just go and do your work."

Uzair remained calm and continued, "There was a small family—a sweet little sister, a wonderful mother, a dashing father, and an older brother. One day, the father died in an accident. Unable to cope, the mother suffered heart attacks and died as well. The elder brother and his little sister were left alone. One day, while the sister was drawing, she fell asleep in her brother's arms. When he awoke, she had passed away in his arms. The brother continued to live alone, battling his fears. This story is mine. I lost everything but never complained. And losing a friend makes you so weak."

He paused, tears streaming down his face. He looked into my eyes and said, "I lost everything, yet I never cried. I don't know why I'm crying now."

Uzair approached the river, washed his face, and said, "Come on, brother, the shop is open. Let's go."

As we walked to the shop, I thanked him, "Thank you for explaining the meaning of life to me."

He placed his hand on mine and asked, "What do you understand about the meaning of life?"

I replied, "Facing difficulties."

He smiled and said, "You don't understand yet. Let's go."

I asked, "If what I said isn't the meaning of life, then what is?"

Uzair placed his hand on my shoulder and said, "Life is about sacrifice and adjustment."

His answer surprised me. "What do you mean by sacrifice and adjustment as life? I don't understand."

Uzair explained, "Because this is not the real meaning of life. Time will reveal what life truly is. Now let's go to the shop. There's no one there."

When we arrived, Uzair acted as if nothing had happened. I asked, "Uzair, don't you remember crying a while ago? Why are you acting as if nothing happened?"

He looked at me and said, "Yes, I was crying, but why should I dwell on it? Remembering the past won't change anything. It will only bring more pain and anger without healing the wounds. Everything is temporary, but you can choose to make it last forever if you dwell on it. Instead of crying, it's better to focus on something more constructive. It's up to you whether you want to cling to pain or seek success. Remember, sometimes bad things happen that we can't even imagine or forget. In those cases, think of it as a dream you've awoken from. Now, a new and beautiful life awaits you. Embrace it fully."

I stared at Uzair, surprised by his depth of understanding. I had always seen him as a weak, fearful boy, but his words revealed a profound wisdom.

CHAPTER SEVEN

The following morning, I woke up early, washed my face, and stared at myself in the mirror. I was troubled by the thought of how Lucy had treated me and how everyone at school had witnessed it. What would I say to them? As I mulled over these thoughts, Uzair's words came back to me: "Forget and remember that what happened until now was a dream." Embracing this mind-set, I resolved to move forward and headed to school without fear.

When I arrived in the classroom, Uzair was already there. As I walked towards him, Lucy stood up and loudly announced, "Hey, look who's here—the friend of an orphan." Her words stung deeply, and in a moment of rage, I slapped her hard. Immediately after, I fled the classroom and ran to the forest. There, I pounded the ground with my fists, berating myself for my actions. "What did I do? I slapped her. Even though it was her fault, she broke my heart, and now I'm crying for her. Why am I doing this?" I wondered. I couldn't make sense of my behavior.

After some time, I went home and later, on Sunday morning, I went straight to the shop. I found Uzair there and headed to the river. Sitting by the riverbank, Uzair joined me and placed a comforting hand on my shoulder. I asked him softly, "What happened after I left?"

He replied, "Nothing much. Lucy was crying, and no one was comforting her. Everyone was busy with their own things, so I comforted her. Did I do something wrong?"

I shook my head. "No, you did well. Let's head to the shop."

When we stood up and looked back, Lucy was already standing there. I braced myself for revenge, but to my surprise, she apologized to me. I was so taken aback that I foolishly trusted her again and forgave her. Soon after, we became friends again, but something didn't feel right. My eyes saw her presence, but my heart felt that she was still distant, as if she had become a stranger to me. I was puzzled by these conflicting feelings. My heart kept whispering, "She's not yours anymore," but when she was near, I couldn't understand why she couldn't be mine. It was all confusing and beyond my grasp.

One day, I was heading to the river when I saw Uzair already sitting there, looking unusually quiet. I approached him and placed my hand on his shoulder. He quickly stood up, wiping away tears. I was shocked; Uzair wasn't someone who usually cried. I placed both hands on his shoulders, concerned, and asked, "Why are you crying?"

He replied, "It's nothing. I was just thinking about my mother."

Realizing I shouldn't have pride, I lowered my head. Then Uzair spoke again, "You know, I fell in love too."

I was astonished. "When did this happen? Tell me your story."

We sat down, and Uzair began to recount his tale. "Once upon a time, there was a boy who believed in love but had a broken heart. He went through many trials. Then he met a girl who captured his heart and healed his wounds, showing him that love could be beautiful again. Their love faced many obstacles— distance, misunderstandings, and personal struggles. Yet, their love remained strong. They fought through every challenge together. Their story became a testament to love's enduring power, despite time and distance. Distance may separate us physically, but it cannot sever our hearts.

It's not always that a girl cheats, sometimes a boy does too, and sometimes neither is at fault. A small mistake can turn into a big problem, and often, these problems are not as huge as they seem; it's the lack of understanding that makes them appear insurmountable. We boys have a bad habit of not revealing our true selves initially. We worry that if we show our real selves too soon, we might be rejected. So, we hide our flaws until we feel secure, and then, when we start showing our true colors, it overwhelms the other person. This lack of honesty can lead to misunderstandings and heartache.

This is why many youths are struggling today—some are distressed, some are sad, and others feel lost. I did something similar, which is why she's not with me now. It's not always the boys who are at fault; sometimes girls are too. If we make someone a friend, we should be upfront about who we are from the beginning. It's crucial to be honest, so the other person knows what to expect. Revealing our true selves later only leads to more problems."

Uzair's words hit me hard. I had thought I was the only one struggling with these issues, but his experience mirrored my own in many ways. His advice about honesty and understand- ing was a revelation. I realized that my own struggle with Lucy was part of a larger pattern of misunderstandings and lack of communication.

I needed to learn from Uzair's story and apply these lessons to my own life.

As we walked back to the shop, I felt a renewed sense of clarity and resolve. I understood that moving forward meant not only accepting the past but also learning to be honest and open in my relationships.

CHAPTER EIGHT

Uzair's words had left a deep impact on me, but he wasn't finished. "Nile, what I'm trying to convey to you is crucial. In everyone's life, there's a period we

call 'teenage.' It's like soft dough—malleable and shape able. Once it hardens, it's much harder to mould. This is a time when if you seek the good, you'll get better; if you lean towards the bad, you'll get worse. It's an age where we often think we know it all, that we don't need anyone's helped, and that our parents are just obstacles in our path. We might feel like they're against us, and that their advice is misguided. Relationships, friendships, and attractions become confusing and challenging.

One of the greatest challenges of this age is loneliness. Even if we say we enjoy being alone, the truth is, we don't. True loneliness is not being surrounded by people who don't talk to you; its being in a crowd and still feeling isolated because the one person who matters to you isn't speaking to you. My mother taught me about loneliness—real loneliness is when you feel alone even in a crowd.

To combat this, we should find someone or something to share our thoughts and feelings with—a friend, a family member, a pet, nature, or anything that can offer companionship. If none of these are available, we should focus on taking care of ourselves and our well-being. Explore new hobbies, engage in activities you enjoy, and you might meet like-minded people who could become great companions. Loneliness is tough at first, but over time, it can become a source of strength and self-discovery.

We should also strive to keep our lives as private as possible. There's no need to share every detail of what we're doing. If someone wants to stay in your life, they will; if not, they will leave. Life is personal, and you don't owe anyone a detailed account of it. When asked about your life, you can set boundaries and assert your privacy.

Another challenge we face is the pressure of peers. Let me give you an example: Imagine you're in a group where everyone starts smoking, and they try to convince you to join them. They might say, 'Come on, just try it once,' or 'It's not a big deal; everyone's doing it.' It's crucial to remember that you have the power to make your own choices. Peer pressure is real, but it's important to stay true to you.

As we navigate our teenage years, let's remember that every stumble is a chance to rise stronger, every setback a lesson in resilience, and every dream a beacon of hope. Let's stand tall, embrace our individuality, and work towards shaping a future that we're proud of. Here are to us—the boys of today, the men of tomorrow. Let's make our mark, chase our dreams, and light up the world with our unique spark. Cheers to the journey ahead—may it be filled with adventure, growth, and friendships that last a lifetime."

"Listen, Nile," he said, looking serious. "Life isn't just about fleeting moments. It's temporary, and you have to make the most of every second. Don't take friendships for granted. They are the foundation of who you are and will be. True friends will be there through thick and thin, and it's essential to cherish those bonds."

Uzair leaned in closer, his expression serious. "You also need to understand that the world isn't always kind. There are harsh realities out there, including the terrible issue of consent and respect. Always remember that true strength lies in kindness and standing up for others. Protect yourself and those around you from harm."

His words hung in the air as I absorbed them, realizing how crucial it was to navigate my feelings thoughtfully. Life was a delicate balance of moments and connections, and it was important to learn from every experience.

His words resonated deeply with me. I turned to Uzair, feeling a profound sense of gratitude. "Today, you've explained things to me in a way no one else has. I hope everyone finds a friend like you. Finding a friend like you is rare. You're like a brother to me, always looking out for me. Thank you."

We both stood up, and I hugged him tightly. It was a moment of genuine connection and appreciation. After the hug, I made my way home, feeling lighter and more hopeful about the future.

CHAPTER NINE

When I returned home after talking to Uzair, I was greeted by a stark and painful reality: my mother's health had deteriorated severely. Without a second

thought, I packed my bag and rushed to be by her side. We had spent nearly four years together, and during that time, our financial situation had improved. But now, the looming shadow of illness cast a heavy weight on my heart.

One day, my aunt called with some exciting news. "Kevin is arriving the day after tomorrow. Come home today so we can pick him up at the airport together." The thought of Kevin's arrival brought me joy. It felt like a glimmer of happiness amidst the recent challenges. I hurried back to my maternal grandparents' place, eager to share the news with Uzair.

I went straight to my shop to surprise Uzair. His face lit up with joy at my arrival. We decided to head to the riverbank to catch up. I was bubbling with excitement about Kevin's return when, out of the corner of my eye, I noticed Lucy on the opposite shore with someone else. It was as if the sky had fallen on me. My heart sank as I watched them. Uzair must have seen the shock on my face because he gently pulled me away from the scene.

"I was about to tell you," Uzair said, his voice soft but firm. "Lucy is with someone else. I don't know much, but it looks like it might be a childhood friend of hers. I wanted to spare you the pain. I'm sorry."

Before I could respond, my aunt called again. "Do you know Kevin's flight has landed? I misheard the time. Come home quickly, and let's decorate for his arrival."

Uzair offered to come with me, and we hurried back to the house to prepare. Despite my efforts to smile and help with the decorations, I was deeply troubled. Kevin's arrival was supposed to be a beacon of joy, but my heart was heavy with the weight of what I had just seen.

As darkness fell, everything was ready. The house buzzed with anticipation, but Kevin was still missing. His phone was off, and worry began to creep in. Uzair was beside me, engrossed in his phone, when he suddenly said, "Oh my God, a young boy had a terrible accident. They say he died— how tragic."

My heart raced as I snatched the phone from Uzair, trying to make sense of the news. The images flashed across the screen, and panic gripped me. Uzair noticed my distress. "Nile, is everything okay? Why did you throw the phone?"

His voice grew solemn as he guessed, "Is it Kevin?"

Tears streamed down my face as I struggled to speak. Uzair, understanding the gravity of the situation, tried to console me. "Buddy, don't worry. Everything will be alright. Be patient."

The real struggle was breaking the devastating news to my aunt, who was eagerly waiting outside. With a heavy heart, I approached her. She held my hands, her eyes brimming with excitement.

"What's wrong? Call Kevin and tell him to hurry. We've been waiting so long."

Before I could say anything, an uncle shouted from the crowd, "Kevin has passed away in an accident."

My aunt's face fell, her grip on my arms tightening as tears streamed down her cheeks. Her voice, choked with grief, was almost unbearable. "Are you trying to trick me? Call Kevin now and tell him to come home."

Unable to hold back any longer, I embraced her, both of us sobbing uncontrollably. The ambulance arrived soon after, bringing Kevin's lifeless body. The scene was heart-wrenching. We cleaned and prepared his body for burial, laying him to rest in the corner of the house.

During this difficult time, my mother called me. "Son, many people come and go in this world. It's important to understand that no one stays forever. Even your father is gone. You need to bear this loss and move forward in life. If we don't strengthen ourselves and endure our pain, how will we handle it? The sorrow of losing loved ones and the loneliness that comes with it will make us stronger. Remember this and take care of everyone around you."

Her words, though painful, filled me with a sense of resolve. I took care of everything, finding the strength to support my family.

Later that night, I received a call from Uzair. There was no network, so I moved closer to the window. As I looked out at Kevin's grave, I saw a figure draped in white, adorned with black dots. She had long, curly hair and wore earrings that made a sweet, melodious sound. She looked beautiful even in the darkness, but when I tried to approach her, she vanished.

Confused and troubled, I went to sleep. The next morning, I woke up and went straight to the shop. I wanted to tell Uzair about the mysterious figure, but instead, I found Lucy there with someone else. My heart shattered all over again.

The scene was not bearable so I moved towards home Standing near the window in my room, memories of Lucy

played like a haunting slideshow. Each moment we shared lingered in my mind, the echoes of her laughter and warmth creating a bittersweet ache in my heart. Suddenly, someone tapped me on the shoulder, pulling me from my reverie. I turned to find a girl with stylishly cut hair that framed her face perfectly, accentuating her lovely features.

Her sparkling eyes held a captivating depth, shining with an energy that instantly drew me in. The way she wore her earrings—a delicate pair that dangled playfully—added a touch of elegance to her already stunning appearance. She had a vibrant smile that seemed to light up the room, radiating a warmth that made my heart flutter.

There was something magnetic about her presence; she exuded confidence and grace, a combination that was utterly enchant- ing. Every detail, from the way she carried herself to the subtle hints of her fragrance, left me utterly mesmerized. It was as if she walked right out of a dream, and in that moment, I felt a spark of admiration blossom within me.

As I gazed at her, I couldn't help but appreciate the beauty not just in her appearance, but in the way she seemed to embrace life with open arms. Her laughter, her kindness, and the warmth of her spirit made her even more captivating. In that instant, I felt a rush of affection welling up inside me—a deep appreciation for the magic she brought into the world.

"Hello, who are you? What are you doing in my room?" she asked, startled, her brows slightly raised.

I blinked, confused, then realized with a jolt that I had walked into the wrong room. Embarrassed, I began to step back toward the door. "I—uh—I'm sorry. I didn't mean to—"

Before I could leave, she stopped me with a curious smile. "Wait. First, tell me who you are. I've never seen you around here before."

Clearing my throat, I explained, "I've been living here since childhood. This is my aunt's house. Who are you?"

Her expression softened. "I'm Lily. Kevin's younger sister."

My jaw almost dropped. **Kevin's sister?** The same Kevin I grew up with, the one who had always been by my side like an older brother. I stared at her, stunned. "You're Kevin's sister? I can't believe it. That means we're cousins!"

Lily's laughter was like the chime of wind bells, light and soothing. She extended her hand, her smile warm and genuine. "Yes, I'm Lily. Nice to meet you."

I shook her hand, feeling a strange sense of comfort wash over me. "I'm Nile. It's good to meet you,

Lily. Can we talk for a bit? We've just met, and I think we should get to know each other."

Her lips curled into a smile, one that felt like the sun cutting through a clouded sky. "Sure," she said, gesturing to the bed. We sat down together, the awkwardness fading between us.

"So, I've never seen you around. Where have you been all this time?" I asked.

Her smile dimmed slightly, and a shadow crossed her features. "I was sent to London when I was little. I've lived there ever since. I only came back recently... after hearing about Kevin." Her voice cracked, and tears welled in her eyes. "I still can't believe he's gone. It feels like I'm living in a nightmare."

Without thinking, I reached out and gently wiped the tears from her cheeks. "Hey," I whispered. "I know it hurts. But I promise, Lily—I'll take care of you. I'll be here for you, more than Kevin ever could. You won't be alone. I'll do everything I can to keep you happy. That's my word."

For a moment, she searched my face as if weighing the sincerity behind my words. Then a soft, playful grin replaced the sadness. "Wow, Nile. What a sweet talker! At this rate, you'll make me so happy I might get fat from all the compliments."

I laughed, and so did she—a real, lighthearted laugh that made both of us forget our pain, if only for a moment. The room felt a little brighter, and the weight on our hearts eased just a little.

We spent some more time together, talking about everything and nothing. When the night grew late, I finally excused myself and returned to my room, my mind swirling with a strange mix of emotions—grief, comfort, and a newfound connection with someone I had only just met.

That night, sleep didn't come easily. Thoughts of Kevin haunted me, but Lily's presence felt like a soothing balm against the ache in my heart.

The next morning, after calling my mom and trying to reach Uzair with no success, I got dressed and went downstairs. I found Lily in the kitchen, playing with an old set of plastic kitchen toys, her expression lost in a sea of happy memories.

She looked so carefree, like a child revisiting a simpler time when life wasn't weighed down by sorrow. I leaned against the doorway, watching her, a small smile creeping onto my face. In that moment, I realized something—Lily wasn't just Kevin's sister. She was someone I wanted to protect, someone I wanted to keep smiling, no matter how dark life became.

I approached her softly and asked, "Can I join you?"

She looked up, her eyes carrying both warmth and sorrow. "Of course," she said, moving over to make space. "Kevin and I used to play this together. It's my way of keeping his memory close."

I smiled and sat beside her, carefully picking up a plastic spoon from the toy set. As we played, I could sense how deeply these moments with Kevin were etched in her heart. Each movement felt like an unspoken tribute to the brother she missed.

Suddenly, my phone buzzed—it was Uzair. "Lucy's at the shop," he said casually. That was all I needed to hear. Without a second thought, I stood up. "I'll catch you later, Lily," I whispered. She nodded, her smile kind and understanding.

I sprinted toward the shop, hope fluttering in my chest. Maybe today I'd finally get to talk to Lucy, maybe this time would be different. But when I arrived, the shop was empty. Lucy was already gone.

Uzair stood behind the counter, raising a brow at my panting form. "You took a while. She left just before you got here."

The disappointment hit me like a punch to the gut. I leaned against the counter, feeling crushed by the weight of missed chances. "Why is this happening to me?" I muttered under my breath, my voice raw with frustration. "Sometimes, Uzair... I just wish I could disappear. It feels like nothing ever goes right."

Uzair put a hand on my shoulder, his gaze calm yet serious. "Listen, Nile," he said quietly, "do you really want to die before your time? Or do you want to live a life so meaningful that when death comes, the world remembers you? Think about it. If you leave now, people will cry. They'll grieve for you. But grief fades. What doesn't fade is legacy. If you live well, your story will outlast your lifetime. People will talk about you with pride—forever."

His words hit deep, sinking into the cracks in my heart where self-doubt and sorrow lived. I pulled him into a tight hug, grateful for the steady friend that he was. For a moment, everything felt still, like a brief sanctuary from the storm raging inside me.

After leaving Uzair, I wandered aimlessly into the jungle, the silence around me mirroring the chaos within. With every step, memories flooded my mind—Kevin's laughter, Lily's tears, and the elusive warmth of Lucy's presence.

I stayed there until the sky bled into darkness, letting the quiet hum of the forest soothe me. It felt as if the trees, the stars, and the night itself knew my burdens and were silently urging me to keep going.

Eventually, I made my way back home, my heart heavier but my mind a little clearer. As I walked through the dim streets, Uzair's words echoed in my thoughts. *Live so that even after you're gone, people remember your name with pride.*

And in that moment, I made a promise to myself—no matter how lost I felt, I wouldn't let life defeat me. I would create a story worth telling, even if it meant crawling through every dark moment along the way.

CHAPTER TEN

It was quite late when I finally reached home. Without bothering to eat, I went straight to my room and sank into the chair, my mind tangled in thoughts. Everything

felt heavy, as if the silence around me carried the weight of unresolved emotions.

A soft knock interrupted my spiraling thoughts. I looked up to see Lily standing at the door. "May I come in?" she asked gently.

I gave a nod, and she slipped inside, her presence comforting in a way I hadn't expected. She sat down on the edge of the bed, brushing her hair behind her ear. "You disappeared so suddenly earlier. I got worried," she said softly. "Is everything okay? You know, if something's bothering you, you can talk to me."

I sighed and leaned back, my gaze drifting toward the ceiling. "What can I say? It's a long, pointless story. You'd probably fall asleep halfway through my tragic little life."

Her warm smile reached her eyes. "Don't say that. You might think your life is stupid, but it isn't. It's part of you—a gift you need to cherish, no matter how broken it feels."

I stood up and wandered to the window, staring at the moonlight spilling over the quiet street. "I'm not ready to talk about it yet," I admitted. "Some things need time to be told, and this is one of them."

Lily's gaze softened, and she stood too, sensing my reluctance. "That's okay. When the heart feels too heavy, it's better not to force words." She paused for a moment, then smiled. "How about I make you a cup of coffee? Maybe it'll help clear your head a little."

I turned to her, surprised by her thoughtfulness. "How do you know that would make me happy?" She grinned playfully. "Call it intuition." With that, she headed toward the door. "Wait here. I'll bring it in a minute."

As she left the room, my phone buzzed. Uzair's name flashed on the screen. "Don't worry," he said on the other end. "We'll figure out what's going on with Lucy."

I exhaled heavily. "Forget it. She's not in my fate, Uzair. It's just not meant to be."

Just as I ended the call, I heard a sudden crash from the hallway. My heart dropped. I rushed out to see Lily standing frozen, wide-eyed, next to a shattered coffee cup. The liquid spread across the floor like spilled ink.

"Lily!" I exclaimed, hurrying to her side. "Are you hurt? Did you burn yourself?"

She shook her head quickly, her face pale. "No, no, I'm fine. I just... I lost my balance for a second."

Something flickered in her eyes—something more than just embarrassment—but I didn't press her. "It's okay," I said gently. "It's just a cup. Don't worry about it."

Her hands trembled as she handed me another fresh cup she had brought along. "I'll head to bed now," she whispered. "It's late. Drink this and try to rest, okay?"

"Thanks, Lily," I murmured, watching her retreat down the hall. I took a sip of the coffee, letting its warmth sink into me, though it did little to ease the storm in my mind.

That night, sleep eluded me, and my thoughts swirled like restless shadows.

The next morning, a knock pulled me out of the little sleep I had managed. I opened the door to find Lily standing there, holding another cup of coffee, her smile as radiant as the sun peeking through the windows.

Chapter Ten

"Morning," she greeted cheerfully, handing me the cup.

I took it with a grin. "How do you always seem to know exactly what I need?"

She gave a soft laugh. "Maybe I have a talent for it."

An idea sparked in my mind. "Hey, how about I show you my shop today? It'll be fun."

Her face lit up with excitement. "Really? I'd love that! Just give me a minute to get ready."

When she returned, she looked breathtaking. Dressed in a black top and light blue jeans that fit her perfectly, she seemed to carry a quiet elegance with her. Her hair shimmered as it caught the morning light, and her bright eyes were filled with anticipation.

I couldn't help but admire her as we walked side by side toward the shop. Her presence felt like a breeze on a stifling day— unexpected, refreshing, and exactly what I needed. Every step we took felt lighter, as if life was hinting that brighter moments were still possible, even when burdened by the past.

As we walked, Lily turned to me, her voice soft yet curious. "If you don't mind, can you tell me more about Lucy?"

I took a deep breath, gathering my thoughts. "Lucy is… like a storm that swept through my life. There was a time when I felt completely alone—abandoned by everyone I thought cared about me. Then Lucy appeared. She was like a ray of sunlight

ACCEPTING THE DARKNESS

breaking through the darkest clouds. For a while, everything felt brighter. We became close, and, before I knew it, I fell for her."

I paused, feeling the weight of those memories. "But just when I thought I was ready to tell her how I felt, she grew distant, cold even. Our friendship withered, and eventually, she left— without explanation, without closure. It's like she disappeared, leaving behind nothing but unspoken words and unanswered questions. Moving on… it hasn't been easy."

Lily listened quietly, her expression filled with understanding. After a moment, she said, "You mustn't let that hold you back. A broken heart feels like it's screaming, but really, it makes no sound. Life, however, keeps moving forward—and so must you."

She stopped mid-step, turning to face me, her brown eyes glimmering with warmth and quiet wisdom. "A broken heart might laugh and dance, even when it's hurting. It's not about pretending you're okay—it's about finding the strength to keep going. You fall, you get back up. The road ahead is long, but every step forward matters."

Her words wrapped around me like a blanket on a cold night, comforting and grounding. I took her hand, grateful for the sense of calm she brought into my stormy world. "Thank you, Lily. I didn't realize how much I needed to hear that."

We walked on, side by side, until we reached the shop. Inside, I gave her a quick tour, proudly showing her everything, and

Chapter Ten

introduced her to Uzair, who greeted her with his usual playful charm. We spent the afternoon talking, laughing, and sipping tea as if the weight of my troubles didn't exist. For a little while, I felt lighter—like I could breathe again.

As the sun dipped low on the horizon, Lily suggested we head to the riverside. It was a place where I often went to find peace. We sat quietly by the water, watching it ripple under the fading light.

"It's getting late," she said, brushing back a strand of hair from her face. "Mom's going to be worried. We should head back."

"You're right," I agreed. "Let's go."

On our way home, Lily suddenly stopped in front of a small park and tugged me toward a wooden bench nestled under a tree. "This is one of my favorite spots," she said with a smile. "I come here often to think. Watching the kids play reminds me that life isn't perfect, but it keeps going. They fall, they cry, but they always get back up—and they never stop playing."

She turned to me, her gaze both serious and kind. "You need to do the same. Lucy was part of your story, but she's not the whole book. Your future doesn't end with her—it begins with you. And no matter what, I'll be here. Our friendship... it's something I cherish. I hope you will too."

Her words felt like a lifeline, anchoring me in the present.

We returned home, where Aunt greeted us with a playful scolding for being out so late. After dinner, Lily and I said our goodnights and retreated to our rooms.

That night, lying in bed, I replayed Lily's words in my mind. For the first time in a long while, I felt a flicker of hope, small but steady.

Maybe, life wasn't about waiting for the storm to pass—it was about learning how to dance in the rain.

CHAPTER ELEVEN

The next day, after waking up and having breakfast, I sat down to study. But something felt off. My thoughts were scattered, and no matter how hard I tried, I couldn't focus. Something was missing. It hit me—Lily hadn't brought me my morning coffee like she usually did. That small ritual had become so comforting that its absence gnawed at me. I glanced at the clock, wondering where she could be.

Unable to ignore the unease growing inside me, I headed downstairs and found my aunt in the kitchen. "Aunt, where is Lily? She didn't bring me coffee today."

My aunt gave me a curious glance. "She left early this morning. I'm not sure where she went."

A strange worry settled in my chest. Lily leaving without a word wasn't like her. I grabbed my jacket and decided to go out and look for her, my mind racing with possibilities. I wandered through all the familiar places we'd visited together, but there was no sign of her. Just as I was about to give up, I remembered her favorite park—the one she had shown me before.

When I reached the park, I saw her sitting alone on the bench, her head slightly bowed, lost in thought. I approached quietly, the crunch of leaves under my shoes barely audible. A playful idea sparked in my mind, and I gently covered her eyes with my hands from behind.

She paused for a moment, her fingers softly brushing against mine, trying to guess who it was. The warmth of her touch sent a shiver down my spine. Then, with a gentle smile, she whispered, "Nile, I know it's you."

I grinned and slid onto the bench beside her, taking her hand in mine. "You seem troubled," I said, my voice soft. "Tell me what's on your mind. You know I'm here for you. Sharing will help, I promise."

She gave me a gentle smile, though her eyes carried a hint of sadness. "No, I'm not sad, Nile. Just… thinking about life. Things at home are hard. Mom hasn't been well, and it's tough. But being sad doesn't change anything, does it? Life has to be lived freely, without letting sadness take over."

I placed my hands on her soft cheeks, looking into her eyes with sincerity. "Lily, I don't let sadness consume me either. But ever since you've been in my life, it feels like the weight

I've been carrying is slowly lifting. With you here, everything feels lighter, better. It's like the shadows in my heart are finally fading."

Lily's eyes glistened under the warm sunlight. She placed her hands over mine, her touch delicate yet steady. "Nile, you don't know how much your friendship means to me. It's become one of the most precious things in my life. I want it to stay this way, no matter what happens."

Her voice softened as she leaned in closer. "Promise me, Nile. Promise me you'll always be there for me, no matter where life takes us."

I squeezed her hand gently, the gravity of her words settling deep in my heart. "I promise, Lily. I'll always be there for you—through every storm, every joy, and every silence in between. You'll never have to face life alone."

We sat there quietly, the world around us humming with the soft rustle of leaves and distant laughter of children. In that moment, nothing else mattered. The chaos, the heartache, the uncertainties—they all faded away. All that remained was the warmth of our bond, the comfort of knowing that we'd found something rare and unbreakable in each other.

I held her hands tightly and said, "Do you think I could ever leave you? I'm yours, Lily. I'll always be there for you, through every challenge and every moment. You'll never be alone. Whenever you turn around, you'll find me standing right behind you. You're a part of me, and I'll never let that change."

She stood up suddenly, a bright smile spreading across her face. "I don't know about life's journey, but let's see if you can beat me in a race home!"

Before I could react, she ran off, leaving me behind. I chased her, taking a different path home, but when I arrived, she was already there, laughing at me. "You lost! You couldn't even beat me in this little race. Life's a long race, Nile, and you're already behind!"

We laughed together, and as we entered the living room, I noticed a beautiful bouquet of flowers in her hands. I smiled at her and said, "You always find a way to make me feel special, Lily."

She blushed and replied, "You deserve it, Nile. I hope our friendship never changes. I want it to stay like this forever."

I took her hands in mine and said, "I feel the same way. No matter what happens, let's promise to always communicate and work things out."

The rest of the evening was spent talking and laughing, making plans for the future. As the night drew to a close, we said goodbye with a promise to meet for breakfast the next day.

In the morning, I woke to the sound of my bedroom door opening. It was Lily, holding a steaming cup of tea. She smiled and said, "Good morning, sleepyhead. I brought you some tea to start your day."

I gratefully accepted the cup, feeling its warmth spread through my hands. "Thank you, Lily. You always know how to make me feel special."

We sat together on the edge of my bed, sipping tea and enjoying the peaceful morning. After a while, Lily stood up and walked to the window, staring out thoughtfully. "You know, Nile," she said, "Love is such a strange thing. It's beautiful but also heart- breaking, like riding an emotional roller-coaster."

I joined her by the window. "Yes, love can be like that. It can lift you to the highest highs and drag you down to the lowest lows."

As I looked into her eyes, confusion washed over me. Was this just friendship I was feeling, or was it something deeper? I couldn't help but wonder if she felt the same way.

Later, we went to the shop, where Uzair greeted us warmly. And we sat down for coffee

Suddenly, someone wrapped their arms around me from behind, pulling me into a warm embrace. I knew that scent instantly—Lucy. My heart faltered, the ground beneath me slipping away. A strange storm of emotions flooded me—happiness, sadness, regret—everything merging into one confusing mess.

"Aren't you going to ask me to sit?" she said, breaking the silence with a playful smile. "It's been so long, Nile."

I gestured toward a chair, still trying to steady myself. I went to fetch her a coffee, my hands trembling as I handed her the steaming cup. Lucy gave me a soft smile and said, "Thanks," before shaking hands with Uzair. "You've grown a lot," she remarked, making him grin sheepishly.

Then Lucy's gaze landed on Lily, and in an instant, the atmosphere shifted. Their eyes locked, not with surprise but with something darker—anger, tension, unspoken hostility. It was as if time had frozen between them, a silent duel unfolding. I could feel the weight of their stare pressing down on everyone in the room.

Sensing the storm about to break, I gently placed my hand on Lucy's shoulder to ground her. "Lucy, this is Lily. She's my cousin—and a really good friend of mine."

Lucy's expression darkened, the corner of her lips curving into a smirk. "Oh, you've made new friends and moved on? That's nice—just keep going forward, Nile." Her words stung, a blend of sarcasm and hurt disguised as casual banter.

I opened my mouth to respond, but Lily spoke first, her voice soft yet firm. "He hasn't forgotten you."

Lucy turned sharply toward Lily, her eyes narrowing. "You seem to know a lot about him. And, by the way, if we were talking, what gave you the right to interrupt?"

The tension thickened, the air between them almost suffocating, until Uzair—ever the peacemaker—jumped in. "Hey, you guys want to hear something hilarious? The other day, I almost tripped into a fountain while trying to impress someone. You won't believe what happened next!"

His cheerful tone cut through the tension, and the moment of confrontation fizzled out like a candle in the wind. But beneath the surface, the animosity between Lucy and Lily simmered. They acted like old rivals, exchanging subtle glances that carried unspoken warnings.

After a painfully long silence, Lily stood up abruptly. "Nile, let's go. Aunt will be upset if we're late."

As I stood to leave, Lucy reached out, grabbing my hand. "Wait, let's talk," she said, pulling me toward the riverside. "Do you remember the old days?" Her voice softened as she led me along the water's edge, bringing back memories of our past.

We laughed, recalling the good times, but something didn't feel right. The more time I spent with Lucy, the deeper my confusion grew. I cared for her—maybe I always had—but there was something undeniable about Lily, something that lingered in my heart. I wasn't sure if my feelings for her were just a passing attraction or something far more profound.

While I was lost in thought, Lucy hugged me tightly. "I missed this," she whispered, before stepping back with a sad smile. "Bye, Nile. I'll see you around."

As soon as she walked away, Uzair grabbed my arm and yanked me toward the other side of the river, frustration evident on his face. "Nile, what are you doing?" His voice carried a weight I hadn't expected.

I stared at him, confused. "What do you mean?"

He shook his head with a knowing look. "You're playing with fire, man. Lucy is your past. Lily? She's your present—and maybe even your future. Don't hurt her. She doesn't deserve that."

His words stung, and I knew he was right. Without waiting for more, I went straight to Lily, finding her sitting quietly beneath a tree near our home. I knelt beside her, gripping her arms tightly, unable to hide my frustration. "Lily, did I hurt you? Did I say something wrong? We've always been open with each other. Just tell me if I've done anything to upset you."

She winced slightly, her gaze lowering. "You're holding me too tight, Nile. It hurts."

Realizing my mistake, I immediately let go and stepped back. For a moment, neither of us spoke, the silence heavy between us. Then, taking a deep breath, I knelt on one knee and looked up at her. "Lily, everyone makes mistakes—and I've made more than my share. But you've always been the one who helps me find my way back. Today, I need you more than ever. Please, put your hand in mine and help me build a life filled with happiness. I'll never leave you—not for anyone. I'll always be by your side."

Lily stared at me, her eyes reflecting both uncertainty and hope. Slowly, she placed her hand in mine. "I don't know if this is right or wrong," she whispered, "but I'll stand by you, no matter what. Even if the world is against us, you'll always have me."

Her words touched something deep within me, but they also planted a question in my mind. Why did she think it was wrong to be with me? What doubts was she carrying? I wanted to ask, but I let the thought drift away. It didn't matter. All I knew was that I would do everything in my power to never lose her.

We walked home together in silence, but my mind wandered back to Lucy. Why did she keep coming back into my life, stirring up emotions I thought I'd buried? Was it a sign? Or just a cruel game of fate?

By the time we arrived home, it was dark. Dinner was already on the table, and we ate in quiet companionship. As we finished, Lily stood to leave, but just before she closed her door, she looked at me and said, "You seemed lost in thought today."

She shut the door without waiting for a response, leaving me alone with my tangled emotions. I didn't dwell on her words, though. Instead, I crawled into bed, my mind swimming with thoughts of Lucy. Sleep came slowly, wrapping me in restless dreams.

The next morning, my phone buzzed loudly, dragging me from sleep. It was Lucy. I answered without thinking.

"Good morning! Are you still in bed?" she teased. "Hurry up and meet me downstairs! Let's spend the day together—just like old times."

Without hesitation, I got ready and rushed to meet her. The day passed in a blur as we revisited old haunts, laughing and reliving the past. But no matter how hard I tried, something still felt off, like I was chasing a version of happiness that didn't quite belong to me anymore.

The more I tried to recapture what we once had, the more I realized something profound: "the person I was chasing might not be the one I truly needed anymore."

By the time I got home that evening, darkness had already settled over the sky. I took a long, hot shower, trying to wash away the confusion and guilt gnawing at me. When I returned to my room, a cold cup of coffee sat waiting on my table with a small note attached. It read: **"Good Morning."**

That's when it hit me—I had completely forgotten about Lily. Guilt flooded my chest. I rushed to her room, wanting to apologize, but she was already fast asleep, her face peaceful beneath the soft glow of the moonlight. I stood there quietly for a moment, the words I wanted to say trapped inside me, knowing I had let her down.

The next morning

I knelt in my room, holding a rose, waiting. When Lily entered, holding a fresh cup of coffee, she paused in surprise, her eyes widening. I smiled, trying to lighten the moment.

"What? Did you think I'd leave without saying goodbye?" I teased gently. "You mean more to me than anything else."

Her lips curved into a soft smile as she took the rose. "It's not that late," she whispered. "Have your coffee, and I'll get ready."

We stepped out of the house together, and that's when I saw

Lucy waiting for me in the garden, leaning against a tree with her arms folded. Her expression darkened the moment she saw me holding Lily's hand. She stalked over, her tone dripping with sarcasm.

"Oh, looks like you're trying something new today," Lucy sneered.

"No, Lucy, it's not like that," I said, trying to calm her. "Lily is my best friend. Just like you."

Lucy scoffed, rolling her eyes. "Yeah, sure. Whatever helps you sleep at night."

Ignoring her, I squeezed Lily's hand, and we kept walking. But Lucy wasn't done. She grabbed my arm and dragged me toward the riverside, her voice softening into a nostalgic murmur.

"Do you remember how perfect everything used to be, Nile? Just the two of us... no one in the way?"

Before I could respond, Lily appeared, her expression strained. "Nile, let's go home. I'm not feeling well here."

Lucy snapped, her voice sharp and venomous. "Is Nile your **pet dog** now? Do you drag him wherever you want?"

Lily's face flushed with anger, but her voice remained calm. "I'm not talking to you. He's my best friend. Just leave us alone."

The tension exploded. Lucy stepped closer, her voice a low hiss. "Nile, it's time to choose—me or her. Do you want a life with me or with... your little pet?"

The words pierced my heart like a dagger. I stood frozen, torn between them. "You're both important to me," I stammered. "I can't—"

"Enough!" Lucy shouted. "Decide, Nile! Her or me?" Lily's voice joined hers. "Yes, Nile—make your choice!"

Their voices overlapped, their demands crashing over me like waves. The pressure, the confusion, the anger—they consumed me. And before I realized what I was doing, my hand swung out. **I slapped Lily.**

The sound of the slap echoed through the air, followed by a deafening silence. Lily's eyes welled with tears, but she didn't cry. She just looked at me, hurt and disbelief shining in her gaze.

"Well done," she whispered, her voice trembling. "You've made your choice." Then she turned and walked away without another word, disappearing from my sight—and from my life, or so it felt in that moment.

From a distance, Uzair had seen everything. He stood quietly, his face a mask of disappointment. But he said nothing. He didn't need to. The damage was already done.

Lucy smiled, triumphant, and slipped her arm through mine. "Don't worry," she whispered. "She deserved it. Now, let's spend this beautiful life together."

But I couldn't move. I couldn't speak. A hollow ache filled my chest, drowning out everything else. Without saying another word, I pulled away from Lucy and walked home.

When I got home, the weight of everything crashed down on me. Anger boiled in my chest— not just at Lucy, or Lily, but at myself. I stormed into my room, grabbed my suitcase, and stuffed it full of clothes and books. I didn't even think; I just knew I had to leave.

When I reached the living room, my aunt noticed the suitcase and rushed toward me. "Nile! What's going on? Are you leaving? Is everything okay?"

I stared at her, my voice sharp and bitter. "Are you upset because I'm leaving—or because you're losing your servant?" The words poured out like poison, and I couldn't stop them. "What's wrong with you and your daughter? Just leave me alone! I've had enough. I'm going back to my own home."

Her face crumpled with a mixture of shock and sadness, but I didn't care. I yanked the suitcase handle and marched toward the door. "Take care," I muttered bitterly. "Or don't. I don't care anymore."

And with that, I left.

That day, **everything changed—for both of us.** The bond between Lily and me, once so strong, shattered like glass. The trust, the friendship, the connection we had built over the years—gone in an instant. The choices I made in anger, the words I couldn't take back—they scarred us both in ways I hadn't imagined.

From that day forward, we were no longer the people we used to be. I became someone else— someone colder, harder. And Lily? She became a stranger, too. We had crossed a line that neither of us could ever uncross.

In my desperate search for clarity, I had lost the one person who had always stood by me. I didn't just lose a friend that day—I lost "myself."

As I walked away from the house, the suitcase clutched tightly in my hand, a cold breeze swept over me, as if the universe itself was reminding me of the emptiness I had invited into my life. And for the first time, I realized...

Some choices can never be undone. Some wounds never heal.

And some mistakes—no matter how much you regret them— will haunt you forever.

CHAPTER TWELVE

After twelve years, my life had transformed into something beyond my wildest dreams. I wasn't just surviving anymore—I was thriving. I stood at the

helm of a thriving business empire, with wealth, influence, and power that I could have never imagined during those early, desperate years. Properties in multiple cities bore my name, and I had become someone people looked up to—some even called me a role model. Wherever I went, admiration followed. People shook my hand with respect, whispered my name with reverence.

Happiness wasn't elusive anymore; it had become my reality. It wasn't the fleeting kind that slips through your fingers— it was steady, anchored by success and the peace that comes with knowing you've made it. My past? Buried. So deep, it felt like a distant, fading dream, almost like the story of another person entirely. The struggles, the heartbreaks, the countless sleepless nights—they were nothing but ghosts, and I had shut every door they could return through.

I had changed. Hardened. Evolved. The boy I used to be— the one drowning in confusion, torn between people, hoping for love that only ever seemed to hurt—was gone. And with him, I had let go of the people from that time, too. I didn't care anymore. Not about the past. Not about anyone in it. I told myself that the person I used to be had died along the way, and all that remained was the man I had become.

And you know what? **It felt good.** Not needing anyone. Not waiting for anyone. Just me and my world, exactly how I wanted it.

But the funny thing about the past... it doesn't stay buried for long. Even when you think you've left it behind, it always has a way of finding you—like a shadow you can't outrun. And little did I know, my shadow was about to catch up.

But then, one ordinary day, as I sat in my office, going over documents, my phone buzzed with a message. I almost ignored it, thinking it was something routine. But out of habit, I checked, and what I saw hit me like a wave.

A picture of my old shop.

I stared at it, frozen. The very shop that had once meant the world to me, the shop where I had spent countless days trying to make a living, barely scraping by. And now, here it was on my screen, looking exactly the same as I remembered it. I could almost smell the old wood; hear the creak of the door as customers came in—few as they were. It was like being transported back in time, to a life I had long since left behind. A strange feeling stirred inside me—something between nostalgia and longing. My heart ached,but not in a bad way. It was like a door I thought I'd shut forever was suddenly cracked open again. I couldn't help but smile, and that smile surprised me. I didn't realize how much I had missed that place—how much it had once been a part of me.

For years, I had pushed those memories away, telling myself they didn't matter anymore, that I was someone else now. But in that moment, I realized—maybe I wasn't so far from the person I used to be after all. The idea of seeing that shop again, of standing there where it all began, stirred something deep inside me.

I wanted to go back. I needed to see it again.

So I made the decision. I had to see it for myself. That old shop—the place where my journey began. I couldn't ignore it anymore. I told my assistant to cancel my meetings for the day, grabbed my keys, and got into my car. As I drove, the feeling was strange—almost surreal. I had spent so long running from the past, building a life far removed from those days. And now here I was, willingly heading back to the place where it all started.

As I rolled down the window, a warm breeze hit my face. The cityscape blurred past, but my mind was somewhere else entirely. Memories began flooding back—fast, overwhelming. Each street I passed seemed to pull me deeper into the past. The late nights I used to work, counting the small earnings at that old wooden counter. The smell of coffee and dust that lingered in the air. The faces of a few loyal customers who kept me going when I thought I couldn't do it anymore.

It was all coming back to me, and I wasn't sure how to feel. There was pride, of course. I had come so far since then. But there was something else too—an ache, maybe. A reminder of how hard those times were, how uncertain everything felt back then. I remember standing behind the counter, wondering if I'd ever make it out, if my dreams were too big for a guy like me.

But I had made it. I had more than made it. And yet, sitting there in my car, I felt something unexpected. A strange gratitude for those tough times, for the struggle that had shaped me into who I am now. Without that shop, without those long, difficult days, would I even be here?

I found myself gripping the steering wheel a little tighter. My heart was beating faster, like I was about to face something important, something personal that I hadn't dealt with in a long time. The past that I had buried was resurfacing, and I didn't know whether it would bring peace or stir old wounds.

But one thing was clear—I couldn't stop now. I had to see it, to stand there again and face whatever was waiting for me.

As I drove through the winding roads leading toward my old shop, the trees around me thickened, the city disappearing behind me like a distant memory. The air changed— fresher, quieter. And then, as if the silence itself was calling her name, she came rushing back to me.

Lucy.

I hadn't thought about her in years, and yet, here she was, filling my mind with a flood of memories I'd rather leave buried. She was always a ghost to me, someone I could never quite touch, never reach. I remember the way her gaze would pass over me as if I were invisible, how no matter how hard I tried, I was never enough for her. She never looked at me the way I wanted her to. She was always out of reach, like a dream you wake from just before you can hold it.

As I drove deeper into the jungle, my grip on the wheel tightened. I could feel the bitterness creeping in, that old ache in my chest, the one that came every time I thought of her. Why did I care so much? Why did I let her have that power over me? Even now, after all this time, the memory of her rejection stung in ways I hadn't expected. I don't love her anymore, but that pain, that sense of never being enough—it lingered.

I shook my head, trying to push her out of my mind, but her voice echoed in the wind that slipped through my open window. I clenched my jaw, forcing myself to focus on the road. She's the past, I reminded myself. Just a scar now, not an open wound.

And then I saw it. The shop.

My heart stopped. I hadn't prepared myself for the sight of it, not really. But there it was, standing just as it always had, unchanged by the years. A part of me thought it might look different— abandoned, weathered by time—but no. It was the same. The same old wooden sign hanging above the door, the same creaky steps leading up to the entrance. It was like stepping into a time capsule, back to a life I had left behind.

I let out a long, shaky sigh, the kind that carries more weight than you realize until you hear it. Everything came rushing back. Every moment, every struggle, every doubt. I could see myself inside, younger, worn out, trying so hard to make something of myself. Every creak of those wooden floorboards held a memory. The late nights counting pennies, wondering if I'd even make rent. The mornings when I'd open the door and pray for customers. The failures. The heartbreaks.

Lucy.

The nights I'd stand behind the counter, thinking of her, wondering why I wasn't good enough. I shook my head again, trying to chase those thoughts away, but it was no use. Standing here, looking at this shop, it felt like no time had passed at all. I hadn't expected to feel this…raw. Like the man I'd become had melted away, and I was back to being that same desperate soul again.

I closed my eyes for a second, letting the memories wash over me. I hadn't missed this feeling, but it was impossible to avoid it now. The smell of the old wood, the sound of the wind rustling through the trees nearby—it all came rushing back. I opened my eyes and stared at the shop. It looked the same, but I was different. At least, I wanted to believe I was.

But being here again, I wasn't so sure.

I stepped out of the car, the weight of the past pressing down on my chest, heavier with each breath. The shop had waited for me, unchanged, and now it was demanding something of me. To face it. To face *him*—the man I used to be.

And as I stood there, staring at the door, a painful sigh escaped my lips, one that carried all the things I thought I had left behind.

As I stood there, staring at the shop, the past pressing in on me, I heard a familiar voice—one I hadn't expected to hear after all this time.

"Nile? Is that really you?"

I turned, and there he was. Uzair. The same bright smile, the same warmth in his eyes, like no time had passed at all. My heart lifted in a way I hadn't felt in years. I couldn't help but laugh, the weight of the past falling away as I took in the sight of my old friend.

"Uzair!" I called out, my voice thick with surprise and joy.

He rushed over, arms open wide, and we embraced like brothers who hadn't seen each other in ages. There was a certain joy in the air, a lightness I hadn't expected. All the memories of those tough days seemed to fade as we stood there, grinning like fools.

"I can't believe it," Uzair said, pulling back to look at me. "It's been forever! Look at you, man, all successful and polished!" He laughed, shaking his head. "You never did forget about this place, did you?"

I looked at him, my chest full of warmth. "And look at you! Still hanging around the shop, huh?"

Uzair's smile softened. "Yeah, well, some things you just can't let go of." He gestured toward the shop, the familiar sight of the old wooden counter visible through the door. "I'm a software engineer now, can you believe that? But no matter how far I've come, I find myself coming back here every weekend. It's like… I don't know. I miss the old days, the people, the simplicity of it all."

I blinked in surprise. "You still come here? Every weekend?"

He nodded, his eyes shining with a mix of nostalgia and happiness. "Yeah, I do. I sit behind the counter sometimes, selling a few things here and there, just to feel like I'm part of something bigger. It's not about the money or the work—it's the connection. This shop… it's where we all grew up, isn't it? Where we figured out who we were."

Hearing Uzair say that made me smile in a way I hadn't in a long time. I could feel the joy bubbling up in my chest, a happiness I hadn't expected to find here. It was like a reunion with a part of myself I'd lost along the way.

We walked toward the shop together, and Uzair opened the door like it was nothing—like he had done a hundred times before. Inside, everything was the same. The shelves, the counter, the creaky floor. It was as if no time had passed at all.

"I never could let this place go," Uzair said with a chuckle. "It's funny, isn't it? I've got this big, fancy job now, but when the weekend rolls around, I'm back here, behind the counter, just like old times. It's peaceful. I guess I miss everyone, the way things used to be."

I looked around, my heart swelling with something I hadn't felt in a long time—contentment. Uzair's presence, his joy at still being here, brought a kind of warmth that filled the room. It wasn't just the shop that felt like home. It was the people, the connections, the memories we had all shared.

"You've always been the heart of this place, Uzair," I said, grinning. "And I can't tell you how good it feels to be back here with you."

Uzair clapped me on the shoulder, his laughter filling the air. "Welcome home, Nile. It's good to have you back."

And in that moment, with Uzair beside me and the shop exactly as I remembered, it felt like I was finally home again. The past wasn't a weight anymore—it was something beautiful, something to cherish. And for the first time in a long time, I was happy to be standing right where I belonged.

Uzair's phone rang, breaking through the moment. He glanced at it, then looked back at me with a smile. "I've got to take this. I'll be back in a little bit, alright? Don't go disappearing on me."

I nodded, watching as he stepped out to handle his call. The shop was quiet again, just me and the memories swirling in the air. Slowly, I walked toward the back where we used to make coffee. The old utensils, the mugs, the little counter where I used to stand—it was all still there, just as it had been. My fingers brushed the edge of the counter, tracing the same path I had walked so many times before. And then, without warning, the memories of Lucy hit me, sharp and clear.

I used to make her coffee every morning. She didn't even like coffee, not really, but I made it for her anyway. I used to watch her sip it, waiting for some sign that she saw what I was doing, that she felt the care I poured into every cup. But she never did. She'd take a sip, wrinkle her nose, and set it down, barely touching it again.

I used to think that maybe—just maybe—one day she'd see it. That she'd look at me, and something would click. That she'd realize how much I loved her, how much I wanted her to be happy, even in the smallest of things like a cup of coffee. But she never did. I could've brewed her the perfect cup a hundred times over, and it wouldn't have made a difference.

I sighed, pulling my hand away from the counter. Those moments with her, they were like ghosts now—haunting, but distant. I had loved her so much back then, but looking back, it felt like I was chasing after something that was never real. She didn't see me. Not the way I wanted her to.

With a heavy heart, I turned and made my way outside, my feet carrying me instinctively to the river.

It wasn't far from the shop, just a short walk, but it felt like a lifetime ago that I had been there. The small, quiet river, with its gentle flow, had once been our spot. My spot with Lucy. The place where I first thought we might have something real.

As I approached the riverbank, the memories crashed over me like waves. I could see it all so clearly—the first time we came here together. It was a warm day, the sun casting golden light over the water. We had sat here for hours, talking about everything and nothing, just two people lost in their own little world. I had felt something that day, something deep and real. I thought she had too.

But then, there were the darker memories. The times we came here, and I thought we were building something, only for her to keep me at arm's length. I had been so blind, so caught up in my feelings that I didn't see what was really happening. I didn't see how distant she was, how she was already pulling away long before I realized it.

And then, there was the day she broke everything.

I remember it so clearly, standing right here on this very spot. The sound of the river in the background, the breeze brushing through the trees. I thought we were just having another one of our talks, but then she said it.

"We can't be friends anymore, Nile."

It felt like the ground had been pulled out from under me. I remember asking her why, trying to make sense of it. She had given me some vague explanation, something about growing apart, about needing different things. But I knew the truth—she just didn't care the way I did. I wasn't enough for her. I never had been.

I stood by the river now, staring at the water, and it was like I could still hear her voice in the wind. That same soft voice that had once made me feel alive, now echoing with the weight of a friendship lost. She had walked away from me that day, and I had stood here, alone, watching her leave.

But even after she broke our friendship, even after everything, we had found our way back to this river. I don't know why, but one day, she had reached out to me, and we had come back here, as if trying to fix something that was already too broken to heal. We sat by the water, like nothing had changed, but it had. Everything had changed. And still, I had hoped. Foolishly, I had hoped.

I crouched by the riverbank now, my fingers dipping into the cool water. I could feel the weight of it all—the love, the loss, the confusion. I had spent so long trying to be what she needed, never realizing that what I needed was never going to come from her. This river, this place, it had seen the best and worst of me. It had seen me hopeful, and it had seen me heartbroken. As the water flowed over my fingers, I closed my eyes and let out a deep, quiet sigh. It wasn't just about Lucy. It was about everything—about the boy I had been, the man I had become, and the pieces of my heart I had left behind here, by this river.

As I sat there, crouched by the river, lost in the swirl of memories, I didn't hear Uzair approaching until he was right behind me. His footsteps crunched softly on the grass, and then he spoke, his voice gentle but knowing.

"You still haven't forgotten her, have you?"

I didn't look up at first, keeping my gaze fixed on the water.

I thought I had buried those feelings a long time ago, but the truth was, I never could. It wasn't just about Lucy—it was about everything she represented, everything I'd lost, everything I had failed to be.

"No," I finally said, my voice barely more than a whisper. "I haven't."

Uzair sat down next to me, his presence steady and comforting. He didn't push, didn't pry. He just sat there, letting me sit with my own thoughts. The weight of my confession hung between us, heavy but shared. There was no judgment in his eyes—only understanding.

"You've come a long way since then, Nile," he said quietly, after a moment. "But some things... they stay with you."

I nodded, staring at the river, feeling the truth of his words. Some things never leave you, no matter how much success you find, no matter how far you run from the past. Some scars are just too deep.

And then Uzair shifted, his tone becoming lighter, but still carrying something serious underneath. "By the way," he said, looking at me out of the corner of his eye, "I told my aunt you're back in town."

I looked at him, my heart sinking instantly. His aunt. She wanted to see me?

Uzair nodded, reading the sudden tension on my face. "She wants to meet you. She… she still cares about you."

My mind shot back to that day, the last time I saw her. I had stormed out of her house, angry, irrational. I'd let my temper get the best of me, said things I never should've said. She had always been kind to me, always treated me like family, and I had repaid her with disrespect.

I could still see it so clearly—her standing there in the doorway, watching me leave, hurt and disappointment written all over her face. I had been too proud, too angry to apologize. I had slammed the door behind me and walked out of her life, leaving that bridge burning in my wake.

And now… now she wanted to see me again?

Shame washed over me like a flood. I felt it deep in my chest, the guilt of that day wrapping itself around me. I had left her behind, just like I had left so many things behind, thinking I could outrun the past. But standing here now, I realized how wrong I had been. You can't outrun your mistakes. They follow you, no matter how far you go.

I rubbed my hands over my face, trying to shake off the heaviness that had settled over me. "Uzair," I said, my voice strained, "I don't know if I can face her."

He looked at me, his expression soft but firm. "You have to, Nile. You can't keep running from this."

I let out a long breath, feeling the weight of the years between us, the distance I had put between myself and that moment. I had been young, foolish. I had hurt someone who had cared about me deeply, and I had never made it right. And now, after all this time, she still wanted to see me.

"She doesn't hate you," Uzair said gently. "She just wants to see you. She's always asked about you. Even after everything."

That made my heart ache in a way I hadn't expected. After everything I had done, after the way I had treated her, she still cared. I didn't deserve that kindness. I didn't deserve her forgiveness.

But maybe… maybe it was time I faced it. Maybe it was time I faced her.

I stood up slowly, brushing the dirt from my hands, feeling the weight of the years pressing down on me. "Alright," I said quietly. "I'll go see her."

Uzair gave me a small, encouraging smile, standing up beside me. "It's time, Nile. You've made peace with so many things. Maybe it's time you made peace with her too."

As I walked back toward the shop, my heart pounded in my chest. The thought of seeing her again brought a mix of anxiety and hope. Could I face the woman who had always seen the best in me, even when I had been at my worst?

I had been a fool. The anger I had felt that day was a mask for my own insecurities. I had lashed out, believing I had the right to hurt someone who only wanted to help me. And now, I would have to confront the pain I had caused.

As we walked, I recalled her face, the way her eyes had looked at me with concern, with love. I could still remember the warmth of her embrace, the comfort of her presence. She had always been there for me, and I had turned my back on her. The shame of that moment wrapped itself around me again, tighter than ever.

"I'll go," I said again, more to myself than to Uzair, as I braced for the confrontation ahead. "But I'm scared, Uzair. What if she hates me?"

Uzair shook his head. "She doesn't hate you. She understands. Just be honest with her. That's all she wants."

I nodded, feeling the weight of his words sink in. Honesty. Maybe that was what I had been missing all along.

As I reached the shop, I took a deep breath and steeled myself for the conversation to come. I wouldn't run anymore. It was time to face the past, to face my aunt, and to finally begin to make amends.

As I drove closer to my aunt's house, my heart raced with a mix of excitement and dread. The familiar sight of the house came into view, and I felt an unexpected surge of emotions wash over me. It was as if time had folded in on itself, and I was a boy again, lost in my pain and confusion.

I caught a glimpse of the window where I had spent countless nights staring out into the darkness, tears streaming down my face. I remembered the feeling of suffocation, the weight of my heart as I cried for the things I couldn't articulate. Those moments of despair seemed so far away now, yet standing here, they felt achingly close.

As I turned my gaze away from the window, my thoughts drifted back to Kevin. He had always been my anchor, my rock. I could picture him clearly, with his easy smile and warm laughter. He had been the best cousin anyone could ask for—caring, loving, and always ready to stand by me when the world felt like it was closing in. But then, in a cruel twist of fate, he was gone, taken from us in an accident that had shattered our family. The memory of his absence struck me like a physical blow, and my heart ached with the weight of that loss.

"Are you ready?" Uzair asked, breaking me from my reverie.

I nodded, though my throat felt tight with emotion. I had to remind myself why I was here, what I was facing. With a deep breath, I stepped out of the car, but as I approached the front door, the memories flooded back, each one a reminder of the love that had once filled this space.

The garden was just as I remembered, overgrown but still beautiful in its wildness. It felt like a snapshot of happier times— Kevin and I racing through the flowers, our laughter ringing out, our futures wide open. I could almost hear his voice echoing in the breeze, teasing me about something silly. But those days were gone, and I was left with the ache of his absence, a reminder of the family we had lost and the bonds that had frayed in our grief.

As I reached the door, my heart pounded in my chest. I raised my hand to knock, but before I could, the door swung open, and there she was—my aunt, her face a mix of hope and fear. The moment she saw me, her expression broke, and she stepped forward, enveloping me in her arms.

"Oh, Nile," she cried, her voice thick with emotion. "I thought I'd lost you forever."

I held her tightly, feeling the warmth of her embrace, the softness of her tears soaking into my shirt. I felt her heart beating against mine, and it was as if all the years of distance and hurt evaporated in that single moment. "I'm here," I whispered, fighting back my own tears. "I'm here."

As she pulled back, looking into my eyes, I saw the pain and loneliness etched into her features. "You're just like Kevin," she said, her voice trembling. "When he left, I felt so alone. I didn't know how to keep going without him."

Her words pierced me, a reminder of the gaping hole Kevin's absence had left in our lives. I had never realized how much my aunt had suffered after he died. She had always been strong, holding the family together through the storm, but now I saw her fragility. I felt a swell of grief for her, for Kevin, and for all the moments we had lost.

"I'm so sorry," I said, my voice thick with emotion. "I never wanted to hurt you. I didn't know how to handle everything, and I ran away."

Her tears flowed freely now, and I wiped away a few with my thumb. "You were going through so much," she replied, her voice laced with both sadness and understanding. "But I never stopped thinking about you. I never stopped hoping you would come back."

I took a step back, my heart heavy with remorse. "I should have been there for you, for Kevin… I should have stayed. I'm so sorry for everything."

She shook her head, her eyes filled with love and forgiveness. "It's not too late, Nile. We can find our way back to each other. We have to."

In that moment, standing there with my aunt, I felt a glimmer of hope emerge from the depths of my heart. Maybe I could make amends, not just for myself, but for her, too. Maybe together we could heal the wounds that had festered in our absence.

As I held her close once more, I realized that this was my chance to reconnect, to find solace in family again, and to honor Kevin's memory by embracing the love that remained. It wouldn't be easy, but I was willing to try. I was ready to face the past and build a future—together.

As my aunt kissed my forehead and whispered for me to come inside, a wave of warmth washed over me, like the embrace of a childhood memory. But beneath that warmth, something heavier lingered—a weight that clung to the air like a secret waiting to be uncovered. I hesitated at the doorway, the familiar scent of home wrapping around me, yet stirring an ache I hadn't expected.

Then, like the whisper of a breeze through cracked windows, a voice drifted into my mind.

"You always know how to make me happy," the voice whispered, sweet and gentle.

I froze, the words catching me off guard, setting off a ripple of recognition. My heart tightened as the voice continued, floating just beyond my grasp.

"You deserve it, Nile."

The words were so familiar—too familiar. They tugged at a part of me I had buried long ago, like the sound of a song half-remembered from another lifetime. My chest grew heavy, and I stood there, lost between the past and the present, trying to place the voice dancing just beyond the haze of my thoughts.

I took a hesitant step further into the room, hoping to shake off the feeling. But my eyes fell on something that stopped me cold—a small pot of flowers resting on the windowsill. The sunlight kissed the petals, making them seem almost alive. Bright and vibrant, full of life. Yet all I could feel was the slow, painful stirring of something buried deep within me, now rising to the surface.

I walked toward the flowers, my fingers trembling as they brushed over the soft petals. They felt warm beneath my touch, but the warmth was fleeting, swallowed by a familiar ache building in my chest.

The flowers... They were her favorite. They were Lily's flowers.

Suddenly, everything inside me pulled tight, like the strings of an instrument wound too far. Memories I had tried so hard to forget surged forward, overwhelming me. I hadn't thought about her in so long, and yet here she was—woven into every petal, every breath I took in this room.

I sank into a chair, unable to move, staring at the flowers as if they might reveal her face. My mind struggled, as if a fog clouded my memories. But then I heard it—her voice, faint at first, but growing louder with each passing moment.

"Hey, Nile, good morning!" Her voice, bright and playful, echoed in my mind, pulling me back to a time when things were simpler.

I could almost see her—the sparkle in her eyes, her infectious smile. But the image flickered, like an old photograph worn by time and regret.

"Hey, lazy boy, get up!" Her laughter filled the room, light and full of life.

The floodgates opened, and the memories came rushing in, each one sharper than the last. I remembered the mornings we spent together, the way she teased me, the warmth of her presence—things I hadn't realized I cherished until now. I had loved her, hadn't I? Maybe not the way she had wanted, but I had loved her, in my own foolish, blind way.

I bolted upstairs, the memories chasing me like ghosts. My heart pounded as I reached my old room and shut the door behind me, as if I could lock the past out. But it was too late— the past was already inside, wrapping itself around me, refusing to let go.

Everything was still there—unchanged, frozen in time. On the table beside my bed sat an old coffee cup, exactly where I had left it years ago. I stared at it, my breath catching in my throat as another wave of memories hit me.

Her voice echoed in my mind, vivid and real. "Ah, there's a lot of time left, Nile. Don't rush it."

I could almost see her sitting beside me, her hands wrapped around her own cup of coffee, her smile as soft as the morning light.

"You know, Nile, love is like coffee," she had said one day, her eyes filled with a meaning I hadn't understood at the time. "It's bitter at first, but if you add the right sweetness… it becomes perfect."

Her words were a confession I hadn't seen for what it was, and now, with painful clarity, I understood. All those little moments—her laughter, her teasing, the way she always made sure I was okay—they were pieces of her heart, given freely. And I had missed it. I had taken it all for granted.

I picked up the old coffee cup, my hands trembling. My heart ached with the weight of all the things I never said, all the moments I let slip away. Tears welled up in my eyes, and this time, I didn't stop them.

"I miss you, Lily," I whispered, my voice breaking as the tears spilled over. "I'm sorry. I'm so sorry."

The regret was suffocating, a storm I couldn't escape. I had been too blind, too foolish, and now it was too late. All I had left were memories—her laughter, her voice, the mornings we shared, and the love she had hidden in every small gesture.

Her voice echoed in my mind one last time, gentle and reassur- ing.

"You'll be alright, Nile. You just have to believe it."

But I wasn't alright. I hadn't been alright for a long time. The past I had tried to bury was still here, raw and painful, refusing to fade.

I rushed downstairs, barely able to breathe, my heart pounding in my chest as if it might burst. The memories were too much— her face, her laughter, the coffee, the flowers. Everything about her came crashing down on me, and I couldn't bear it anymore.

"Lily?" she finally whispered, her voice trembling. "She… she left the day you left, Nile."

Her words hit me like a punch to the chest, knocking the wind from me. I staggered, barely able to stand under the weight of them. I couldn't believe what I was hearing. Lily had left too? I thought she might have stayed, that maybe… maybe she would have been here, waiting. But she had gone. Gone because of me.

"I was all alone, Nile," my aunt continued, her voice cracking. "After you left, everything fell apart. Lily was heartbroken, devastated. She waited for you to come back, but when you didn't, she couldn't stay here anymore. She told me she couldn't bear it—the memories, the emptiness."

I felt my knees buckle, my heart twisting painfully in my chest. I had left her. I had left without thinking about what it would do to her, how it would break her. And now, she was gone.

"Where… where is she now?" I asked, my voice barely a whisper, fear tightening in my throat.

My aunt looked away, tears welling up in her eyes. "She went to London, Nile. After you left, she packed up and left for good. She never called, never wrote to us after that. It's been years, and we haven't heard a word from her since."

The world around me spun. London. She had gone so far away, disappeared into a city where I'd never find her, never be able to apologize, never be able to make it right.

"I tried to reach out to her, Nile," my aunt continued, her voice breaking with emotion. "But she didn't want to be found. She was heartbroken. I think… I think she thought you would come back for her. But when you didn't…" She shook her head, wiping at her eyes, her shoulders trembling with the weight of her words. "I lost her too."

Tears burned at the corners of my eyes as the reality of what she was saying sank in. Lily had waited for me. She had hoped I would return, that I would come back for her, but I had been too wrapped up in my own world, too consumed with my own path. I had never looked back.

I collapsed onto the nearest chair, my chest tight, my breaths shallow. All this time, I thought I had left the past behind. But the truth was, I had left her behind. I had walked away from the one person who had always been there for me, who had cared for me more than anyone, and now she was gone—out of reach, maybe forever.

"Lily…" I whispered, my voice shaking with the weight of regret, "I'm so sorry."

Uzair and I sat on the rooftop, staring into the night, the stars scattered above us like distant memories. The air was cool, but my chest burned with the weight of everything that had happened. I took a long drag from the cigarette, exhaling slowly, watching the smoke curl into the night sky. "Why, man?" I muttered, my voice low and full of confusion. "Why did Lily do all this? There's no reason for it. Why didn't she say anything? Why didn't she tell me what was wrong?"

The cigarette burned between my fingers as if waiting for an answer I wasn't sure would ever come. Uzair sat beside me, quiet for a moment, his gaze locked on the horizon. Then, without a word, he leaned over, grabbed the cigarette from my mouth, and flicked it off the roof, watching it disappear into the darkness below.

"You remember everything," Uzair said, his voice calm but laced with something heavier. "But you're forgetting one thing,

Nile."

I looked at him, confused. "What?"

He sighed, his eyes filled with something that resembled both sympathy and frustration. "You don't remember the day you slapped her."

Those words hit me like a punch in the gut. My heart stopped for a moment, and the memories— those painful memories I had tried so hard to forget—came flooding back with brutal clarity. The anger, the frustration, the look on her face when I lost control.

I could see it as clearly as if it had just happened yesterday—her eyes wide with shock, the hurt that flickered there for a split second before she turned away, trying to hide the pain. She hadn't fought back, hadn't yelled at me or said anything. She had just stood there, silent, as if the blow had taken something from her that she couldn't get back.

I hadn't thought about it in years. I had buried it, deep, where I wouldn't have to face the shame of what I had done. But now, it was all I could think about. I had hurt her, in more ways than one, and I hadn't even realized how much until it was too late.

"Yeah," Uzair said softly, "I remember that day. And I remember something else, too."

I couldn't meet his gaze. My throat felt tight, and I was barely holding it together.

"She loved you, Nile," Uzair said, his voice steady but full of emotion. "She loved you more than anyone else. But you were so lost in Lucy, so blinded by your feelings for her, that you couldn't see what was right in front of you. You never saw the way Lily looked at you, the way she was always there, always putting you first—even when it hurt her. Even when it broke her heart."

The words cut deep, each one like a knife, twisting in my chest. Uzair was right. I had been too caught up in my obsession with Lucy, too focused on what I thought I wanted, to see what was real. I hadn't seen the love in Lily's eyes, hadn't noticed the way she tried to hide her jealousy every time Lucy was around. And I had hurt her. Over and over again, without even realizing it.

"I never meant to," I whispered, my voice trembling. "I never wanted to hurt her."

"But you did," Uzair said, his tone firm but not unkind. "You hurt her more than you know. And she never said a word. She kept it all inside, because she loved you. Because she thought you'd come around. But you never did."

I closed my eyes, the weight of regret crashing down on me like a wave. The image of Lily, standing there with her quiet strength, her love hidden beneath a layer of pain, played over and over in my mind. How had I been so blind? How had I let her slip away without even realizing what I was losing?

"I can't change the past," I said, my voice barely audible. "I can't undo what I've done."

Uzair placed a hand on my shoulder, his grip firm. "No, you can't. But maybe it's not too late to make things right."

I looked at him, confused. "What do you mean?"

Uzair's eyes sparkled with something—a mix of hope and determination. "Don't you think it's time you found her? Don't you think it's time you went after Lily, told her what she means to you? She's out there, Nile. Somewhere. And maybe, just maybe, she's been waiting for you to realize that you've loved her all along."

His words hung in the air, full of possibility. My heart pounded in my chest, the thought of it filling me with a strange sense of adventure—an urge to fix what I had broken, to go after the one thing that still mattered.

"But what if—" I started, doubt creeping in.

Uzair cut me off, shaking his head. "You owe it to her, Nile. You owe it to yourself. Stop running from your past. You can't keep burying the things that hurt, hoping they'll go away. Sometimes, you've got to face them head-on."

I stood up, the weight of everything Uzair had said settling in. He was right. I couldn't run anymore. I had to find her. I had to tell her everything, before it was too late.

"Are you coming with me?" I asked, a small, hopeful smile tugging at the corner of my mouth.

Uzair grinned, standing up beside me. "Always, bro. Let's go find her."

And in that moment, I knew what I had to do. We were going to find Lily, no matter where she was. No As the first light of dawn crept through the cracks of the roof, I found myself still awake, thoughts swirling in my mind like leaves caught in a storm. Uzair had fallen asleep beside me, his steady breaths a reminder that I wasn't alone in this. We were on the brink of something big—something that could change everything.

I glanced at Uzair, his face peaceful in sleep, and felt a surge of determination. It was time to find Lily. I needed to get to London, to find her and finally confront everything I had buried for too long. Quietly, I slipped out from under the blanket and tiptoed down the hall, my heart racing with anticipation.

As I approached Lily's old room, I felt a mix of excitement and trepidation. I hadn't stepped inside in years, but now, it felt like stepping into a different world. The door creaked slightly as I pushed it open, and I was immediately enveloped by a wave of nostalgia.

The room was just as she had left it, perfectly decorated with soft pastel colors and twinkling fairy lights. It felt alive, as if she had just stepped out for a moment and would return any second. The walls were adorned with pictures of her smiling, her laughter captured in those frames.

In the center of the room stood a beautiful wooden desk, cluttered with art supplies and sketches. I walked over, running my fingers over the pages. There were drawings of flowers, landscapes, and— most heartbreakingly—a few unfinished sketches of me, with words scribbled beside them. "Always in my heart," one of them read, and my chest tightened painfully at the realization of how much she had cared.

But it was the small diary lying open on the desk that caught my attention. I picked it up, the cover soft and worn, and felt an inexplicable pull to it. As I opened it, the first page made me catch my breath. In delicate handwriting, it read, "My life," and beneath it, my picture was taped—just a simple snapshot of me, but it felt like a piece of her heart.

I turned the page, and the words flowed like a river, each sentence filled with emotion. "It starts from you, Nile," it began, and my heart thudded painfully in my chest. As I continued to read, I saw every moment we had shared captured in her words. Descriptions of our laughter, our late-night talks, and even the moments of silence that felt heavy with unspoken feelings.

Tears filled my eyes as I read her confession of love, the way she had poured her heart into this little book. "You are my sunshine," one entry said. "Every day feels incomplete without your laughter. I wonder if you see it too—the way my heart races when you walk into a room, how your smile lights up my darkest days."

Each line was a reminder of the love I had overlooked, the love that had been waiting for me all along. The realization hit me like a wave, and I felt the warmth of tears spilling down my cheeks as I read about her dreams of a future that included me, about the moments of jealousy that had gnawed at her, the times she had wished I would notice her.

I closed the diary, my heart pounding, overwhelmed by the weight of her words and the memories they stirred within me. This was it. I had to go now, to find her before it was too late. The determination that had ignited in me earlier surged back with renewed intensity. I couldn't let this opportunity slip away.

With tears still in my eyes, I made my decision. I was going to London, to face everything and finally tell Lily what she meant to me. I wouldn't let fear hold me back any longer. I took one last look around her room, feeling the warmth of her presence surrounding me, and then stepped out, ready to take that leap of faith, no matter how far I had to go to make things right.

The next day dawned bright and promising, filled with an energy I hadn't felt in years. My heart raced with anticipation as I prepared for the journey ahead. We had our flight scheduled for 12 PM, and I could hardly believe that I was finally taking this step toward finding Lily.

As I moved through the house, I felt a strange mix of excitement and nervousness bubbling within me. My aunt had been in such high spirits ever since I told her about my plans. She buzzed around the kitchen, making breakfast and humming a cheerful tune, her joy infectious.

"Nile, I can't believe you're really doing this!" she exclaimed, her eyes sparkling. "You've always talked about finding Lily, and now it's finally happening! I'm so proud of you."

Her enthusiasm made my heart swell. It felt good to have her support, especially after all the time we had spent apart. I knew how much she cared for me and how she had always believed in my dreams.

"Thanks, Aunt," I said, a smile spreading across my face. "I just hope I can make things right with her."

"Just be yourself, and remember how much she loves you," she encouraged, pouring a steaming cup of coffee. The familiar aroma filled the kitchen, wrapping around me like a warm embrace.

I quickly packed my things, checking and rechecking my bag as if the act could somehow calm the whirlwind of emotions inside me. I had everything I needed—my passport, a few clothes, and, most importantly, the diary that had reignited my hope.

As the clock ticked closer to noon, my excitement grew. We arrived at the airport, the bustling crowds and the sound of announcements filling the air. I could feel the thrill of adventure in my veins, the sense that I was finally doing something that mattered.

When we got to the gate, my aunt turned to me with a proud smile. "You're going to do great, Nile. Just remember, you've always had the power to shape your own destiny."

I nodded, her words echoing in my mind as I realized how true they were. I was ready to take control of my life, to confront the past, and to reclaim the love that had been waiting for me.

As I boarded the plane, I felt a surge of determination. This was it—the beginning of a new chapter. With each passing moment, I grew more certain that finding Lily would change everything, not just for me but for us both. I settled into my seat, ready to face whatever lay ahead, knowing that I was finally on my way to the girl I had loved for so long.

CHAPTER THIRTEEN

As we settled into our seats on the flight, the hum of the plane filled the air, a steady reminder that we were leaving behind one chapter and flying into another.

I stared out the window, watching the ground grow smaller beneath us, and my thoughts drifted to the journey ahead—and to the mistakes I'd made along the way.

It's funny how life works, especially when you look back on it from the distance of time. As a teenager, I thought I knew everything. I thought the world revolved around my wants, my needs. But as I've grown older, I've realized that life is so much bigger than that. So much more complicated. The choices we make in those reckless, impulsive years have a way of shaping us long after the moment has passed.

I thought of Lily then, and the way I had been so blind to her feelings. My mind had been consumed with Lucy—chasing after someone who didn't care, while the one who did was right beside me, unseen. It's a lesson we often learn too late: the people who care about us are the ones who make the smallest, quietest sacrifices. The ones who stick around, not the ones who dazzle us from a distance.

Mistakes—especially those we make when we're young—can feel like the end of the world. In some ways, they are. They end who we were, leaving us to pick up the pieces of who we want to become. I used to think regret was something to avoid, that it was a sign of weakness. But regret, I've learned, is just another teacher. It's how we know we've grown, how we realize we could've done better. And the beauty of life is that

And the beauty of life is that it gives us second chances—if we're brave enough to take them. Regret doesn't have to be a weight that drags us down. It can be a reminder to move forward with more intention, to treat the people we care about with the love and respect they deserve.

I think about how much time I wasted chasing after things that didn't matter, chasing people who never saw me, while ignoring the ones who did. As teenagers, we're often caught up in the superficial—the thrill of being liked, the excitement of the unknown. But as you get older, you realize that life isn't about the loudest voices or the biggest moments. It's about the quiet ones. The moments that pass unnoticed at the time but stay with you forever.

We make mistakes because we're human. We hurt others, sometimes without even realizing it, because we're still trying to figure out who we are. The important thing isn't that we make mistakes, it's that we learn from them. That we have the courage to face our past and the people we've hurt. That we make amends, even if it's painful.

The teenage years are full of mistakes, of broken friendships and misunderstandings. But that's also where the seeds of growth are planted. It's where we start to understand who we want to be, who we want to have in our lives. And sometimes, like in my case, it takes years to fully comprehend what we've lost or overlooked in those formative years.

As I sat on that plane, thinking about all of this, I realized that facing Lily wasn't just about confronting my feelings for her. It was about confronting who I had been—and who I had become. It was about making peace with the past, and, in doing so, giving myself the chance to create a better future.

Life isn't about avoiding mistakes; it's about learning from them. It's about forgiving yourself for the things you didn't understand then and embracing the wisdom you've gained since. And sometimes, if you're lucky, you get a chance to set things right.

As we soared through the clouds, I felt a strange mix of nervousness and hope. This trip wasn't just about Lily—it was about me, too. About facing the parts of myself I had run from for so long. And maybe, just maybe, finding peace in the process.

The thing about mistakes, especially when you're young, is that they don't feel like mistakes at the time. They feel like choices, moments driven by emotion or impulse. But as the years pass, you start to see them for what they really are: lessons in disguise.

Sitting in that plane, with the hum of the engines and the soft murmur of other passengers around me, I couldn't help but think about how different life is from what I imagined it to be back then. Back when every decision seemed monumental and every setback felt like the end of the world. But as I grew older, I realized life isn't about avoiding failure or heartbreak. It's about how we rise from it.

Teenage years are full of passion, confusion, and trying to find our place in a world that's constantly shifting around us. We push people away, sometimes without meaning to. We chase dreams, often without knowing if they're truly ours. And in all of that chaos, we overlook the quiet, steady things— the ones that matter most.

Lily, I realize now, was one of those things. Her love wasn't loud or demanding. It didn't shout for attention like Lucy's did. It was steady, patient, and always there, even when I was too blind to see it. And that's the thing about love—it doesn't always come in the form we expect. Sometimes it's quiet, almost invisible, until it's too late.

I remember those days when I would bring her coffee, thinking it was just a gesture of friendship, never realizing the depth of what was between us. She never asked for more, never demanded my attention, and because of that, I took her for granted. I was too busy chasing after someone else's approval, too lost in my own world to recognize the love that was right in front of me.

It's funny how much time we spend searching for something we already have, how often we ignore the things that truly matter because we're so focused on what we think we want. And in that pursuit, we lose sight of the things that could have made us happy all along.

Now, years later, I understand the value of those small moments. The coffee, the late-night conversations, the way her eyes would light up when she saw me, even if I was too distracted to notice. It's those moments that stay with you. Not the big dramatic gestures, but the quiet, simple acts of love that we often overlook.

As I sat there, I thought about how much we change with time, how our perspectives shift as we grow older. The things that seemed important at 18—popularity, fitting in, chasing after the wrong people—mean so little now. What matters is the relationships we nurture, the people who stand by us when everything else falls apart. And if we're lucky, we get a second chance to make things right with them.

I've come to understand that forgiveness, especially self-forgiveness, is crucial. It's easy to hold on to guilt, to let it consume you, but at some point, you have to let it go. You have to accept that you were doing the best you could with what you knew at the time. That's how we grow—by facing the mistakes of our past and choosing to be better, to do better, moving forward.

Looking out the window, the clouds stretching endlessly beneath us, I realized that this journey was more than just about finding Lily. It was about finding myself. The version of me that had been lost in all the mistakes and regrets, the one who had once believed in love, in second chances, in making amends. And now, after all these years, I was ready to try.

The past is a part of us, but it doesn't have to define us. We carry our lessons with us, but we also have the power to change the story, to turn regret into redemption. This flight, this trip to find Lily, was my chance to do just that.

As the plane began its descent, I felt a shift, not just in altitude but in something deeper, something inside me. The seat-belt sign blinked on, and I could feel the subtle pressure building in my chest. The ground was getting closer, and with it, a sense of reality—of what was waiting for me on the other side of this journey.

I thought about what it all meant, about the hope I carried with me. Hope is a funny thing. It's fragile, easily shaken, but it's also the one thing that can keep you moving forward when everything else seems to fall apart. Hope is what gets you through the nights when sleep won't come, when regret weighs heavy on your mind. It's what whispers to you that, despite everything, there's still a chance to make things right.

I had spent so much time running—from my past, from my mistakes, from the people I had hurt. But now, as the plane touched down, I realized that running wasn't the answer. Life isn't about moving on and leaving everything behind. It's about carrying those experiences with you, letting them shape you, but not letting them define you. Moving on sometimes means letting go of things that hurt, but it doesn't mean forgetting. It doesn't mean erasing the people who once meant everything.

You can't just push away the parts of your life that are painful. They stick with you. They shape who you are. And maybe, just maybe, that's a good thing. Because the hardest moments in life, the mistakes, the regrets—they teach you more about yourself than anything else. They show you what you're capable of, how strong you are, and where your heart truly lies.

As we landed, I realized that this trip wasn't about leaving the past behind. It was about returning to it. To face it. To make peace with it. It's easy to tell yourself to "move on," to forget the people who hurt you, or the mistakes you made. But real growth comes from facing those things head-on, from understanding them, and from refusing to let them keep you from living the life you want.

Sometimes, we think moving on is the answer, but the truth is, you never really move on from the things that shaped you.

The people, the memories—they're always a part of you. What matters is what you choose to do with them. Do you let them hold you back, or do you use them to build something better?

Hope, I realized, isn't just about wishing for a better future. It's about believing that, despite everything, you can heal what's broken. You can fix what was lost. You can find your way back to the things that matter, even if the path has been long and full of missteps.

As the plane came to a stop and the world outside came into focus, I knew this was my chance. Not to start over, but to continue—to mend the parts of my life I thought were too broken to fix. Life isn't about forgetting. It's about remembering. And in that remembering, finding hope again.

I stood in front of the mirror, my reflection staring back at me, almost like a stranger. The hotel room in London felt cold and unfamiliar, but it was my thoughts that weighed heavier than the room itself. The city outside was alive, buzzing with energy, but all I could hear was the quiet hum of my uncertainty. Uzair had left for dinner, leaving me alone with my thoughts— and with the question that had been haunting me ever since we landed: *Can we really find Lily?*

I looked at myself, searching for answers in the face that had changed so much over the years. The lines were deeper, the eyes a little more tired, but behind all that, there was still a glimmer of hope—however fragile it felt.

What if she doesn't want to be found? That thought hung in the air, heavier than the rest. I knew I had hurt her. I knew I had ignored the love she had quietly offered me while I chased after someone else. But more than that, I wondered if too much time had passed. Could we really bridge the distance created by years of silence, by all the unspoken words and unresolved feelings?

Standing there, I couldn't help but feel a sense of regret—not just for the things I had done, but for the things I hadn't. The missed opportunities, the unsaid apologies, the moments I could have made things right but didn't. And now, after all this time, I was here, trying to make sense of it all, hoping that maybe, just maybe, I could find her.

But hope is a tricky thing. It can make you believe in possibilities, but it can also set you up for heartbreak. I had spent so long running from the past, convincing myself that I was fine, that I had moved on. And now, I wasn't so sure.

I touched the cold surface of the mirror, feeling the weight of everything. *What if she had moved on?* What if I was chasing something that no longer existed? I closed my eyes, trying to shake the doubt. But it clung to me, heavy and relentless.

Then, something inside me shifted. I wasn't that same person who had let her slip away all those years ago. I wasn't the boy who had been too blind to see what was right in front of him. I had changed, and maybe—just maybe—this time would be different.

It wasn't about whether I could find Lily. It was about whether I had the courage to face whatever came next. Whether it was forgiveness or closure, love or loss—I had to try. Because some people are worth fighting for, even after all the mistakes, all the time that's passed.

I opened my eyes, staring at the reflection again. I didn't know if I would find her, or what would happen if I did. But I knew one thing for sure: I couldn't run from this anymore.

Hope is about taking a step forward, even when you're not sure where the road will lead. And that's what I was about to do. I was going to find her—whether she was ready for me or not.

The next day, Uzair and I set out on what felt like an impossible journey. We searched everywhere— colleges, offices, schools—hoping to catch even a glimpse of her. But it was as if Lily had vanished into thin air. The city was vast, and despite our determination, every lead turned into a dead end. All day, we roamed through crowded streets and quiet alleys, chasing the hope that maybe, just maybe, we'd find her somewhere. But at the end of the day, we found nothing.

A week passed, and still, nothing happened. Each day felt heavier than the last, each disappointment weighing me down a little more. London, once filled with the hope of finding her, now felt suffocating. Everywhere I looked, I saw people going about their lives, completely unaware of the search that was tearing me apart inside. My mind was flooded with questions—

Had I waited too long? Was she even in this city anymore? Had I lost her for good?

It was the start of the new week, and we were having lunch at a small cafe when it finally hit me. I couldn't take it anymore. The waiting, the endless searching—it was like chasing a shadow. I pushed my chair back and stood up abruptly, the frustration bubbling over.

"It's over," I said, my voice shaking with anger. "She's not here, Uzair. They lied. There's no sign of her anywhere!"

I felt a surge of bitterness rising in my chest. The idea that all of this was for nothing—that she was out of reach, out of my life for good—was too much to bear. I had poured everything into this, only to hit one dead end after another.

Uzair got up calmly, his gaze steady as he looked at me. He could see the frustration, the doubt, the helplessness. But instead of joining me in my anger, he took a deep breath and said, "Nile, you can't give up just because things get tough. Life doesn't work like that. If you give up now, you'll carry this with you forever. You'll always wonder if you could've found her if you'd just kept going a little longer."

His words hit me hard, cutting through the haze of frustration. He was right. Giving up wouldn't change anything. If I walked away now, I'd be haunted by the same question for the rest of my life: *What if I had tried harder?*

Uzair continued, "Life's not about how many times you get knocked down. It's about how many times you get back up. People give up too easily, thinking that if things don't come quickly, they're not meant to be. But the truth is, the hardest journeys are the ones that matter the most. If you want something, you have to be willing to fight for it—no matter how long it takes."

I stood there, silent, letting his words sink in. He was right. I had come too far to quit now. Lily wasn't just someone I could walk away from. She was more than a memory, more than a lost love. She was a part of me. And if there was even the slightest chance of finding her, I had to keep trying.

Uzair reached over and clapped me on the shoulder. "Come on, Nile. We've got work to do. This isn't over—not by a long shot."

With a new sense of determination, we set off again. The search wasn't easy, and it wouldn't be quick, but I knew I couldn't turn back. Sometimes, the only thing standing between you and what you want is your own willingness to keep going. And I wasn't ready to give up—not on her, not on us.

Uzair and I had been walking for what felt like miles, just trying to clear our heads, to escape the heaviness of our search. He had his headphones in, nodding to whatever music he was listening to, and had wandered off to the side while I scrolled mindlessly through my phone. I wasn't expecting anything— certainly not what happened next.

As I glanced up, my gaze landed on a figure stepping out of a small shop across the street. For a second, the world seemed to freeze. It was Lily.

There she was, just as beautiful as I remembered, but even more striking now after all these years. Her hair, the soft waves that used to fall over her shoulders, glowed under the evening sun. Her eyes, bright and full of life, had that same spark I could never forget. She looked graceful, almost untouched by time, her presence commanding in the simplest way. The way she moved, with that quiet confidence, that elegance—like she didn't have to try to catch anyone's attention, but she had mine. I stood there, breathless, watching her from across the street.

And then, just as I gathered the courage to take a step toward her, I saw him.

A boy, maybe a little younger, walked up to her with an easy familiarity. He smiled, and she smiled back, a soft, genuine smile that I hadn't seen in years. He reached out, placing his hand gently on her back. And the way she looked at him—it was like they knew each other well. Too well. My chest tightened, and I could barely breathe.

I froze, the world crashing down around me. It wasn't supposed to be like this. She wasn't supposed to be with someone else. Not Lily. Not her.

I turned away, feeling the sharp sting of reality hit me harder than I expected. I grabbed Uzair, pulling him from whatever world his music had taken him to.

"Let's go," I muttered, my voice strained.

Uzair looked at me, confused. "What happened?"

I couldn't even speak. "Just… go home," I choked out, turning my back on the sight of Lily with someone else.

Back in the hotel room, the weight of it all collapsed on me. Everything I had hoped for, all the silent wishes, shattered in that one moment. I slammed the door behind me, my mind a blur of anger, regret, and pain. I could hear Uzair outside, banging on the door, yelling for me to open up, but I couldn't. I couldn't face anyone.

Inside, I broke. The walls closed in, and I was left alone with the mess I had created—years of ignoring Lily's love, of chasing after a girl who never loved me back. Every mistake, every bad decision, came crashing down on me at once. My heart ached like it never had before, not just from seeing her with someone else, but from knowing that I had been the one to push her away. I had been so blind, so focused on Lucy, that I never saw what was right in front of me.

I sank to the floor, my back against the door as Uzair's voice faded into the background. My chest tightened, and tears burned in my eyes, but I fought them back. This was all my fault. Every single piece of this heartbreak was my doing.

How had I let it come to this? How had I let the one person who truly cared about me slip through my fingers? Lily had loved me, and I had been too wrapped up in my own selfish desires to see it. Now she was gone. With someone else. And I was left with nothing but the ruins of my own mistakes.

I was broken—broken in a way I had never been before. And the worst part? I had done this to myself.

I packed my clothes in a daze, my heart pounding in my chest as I tried to block out the memory of seeing Lily with someone else. The pain was unbearable, but I kept moving, almost on autopilot, shoving things into my bag. When I opened the door, Uzair was standing there, his face filled with worry.

"Hey, Nile, is everything okay?" he asked, his voice soft but filled with concern.

I didn't answer. I couldn't. My throat felt tight, and the words just wouldn't come out. I was silent, but as soon as he stepped toward me and pulled me into a hug, everything broke. I clung to him like I hadn't clung to anyone in years. The hug, that simple act, was like a release. And I lost it. I sobbed into his shoulder, my tears soaking his shirt, and I yelled, the words spilling out of me like they'd been trapped for too long.

"It's my fault! It's my fault, Uzair! She doesn't love me anymore. She's with someone else now, and I— I can't handle it. I pushed her away, and now she's gone, and I just want to leave this place! Please, just take me away from here. I can't do this anymore."

As I cried, Uzair didn't say a word at first. He just held me tighter, letting me fall apart in his arms. I felt his hand on my back, reassuring, comforting, like he was trying to absorb some of the pain I was carrying. It was as if, in that moment, he knew that nothing he could say would make it better, so he just let me be broken. He let me cry, because sometimes, when you're shattered, that's all you can do.

Uzair finally spoke, his voice steady and calm. "Nile, when we're broken like this, sometimes the only thing we can do is cry. There's no shame in it. You have to let it out. It's part of healing. You can't carry all that pain alone. If you keep it bottled up, it'll only eat away at you."

His words were like a balm to the storm raging inside me. He wasn't pushing me to move on or to forget. He was letting me feel it, letting me grieve for everything I'd lost. And maybe that was the first step—allowing myself to feel the pain instead of running from it.

After a while, when my sobs quieted down, Uzair pulled back slightly and looked at me. "You don't know for sure, Nile. You don't know what's really going on. Are you giving up just because you saw her with someone else? We'll figure it out. We'll find out who he is. But don't make any decisions until you know the full story."

I wiped my face, still feeling raw, but there was a small part of me that wanted to believe him. That maybe, just maybe, things weren't as hopeless as they seemed. But in that moment, all I could think about was the regret. The fear that I had lost Lily forever.

Still, Uzair's words planted a small seed of hope. Maybe this wasn't the end—at least not yet.

Uzair's words lingered in my mind as I tried to pull myself together. He was right—there was too much I didn't know, and my head was spinning with assumptions. Who was that guy with Lily? Maybe he wasn't what I thought he was. Maybe I had jumped to conclusions out of fear and guilt. I wiped my face, trying to get a grip.

"We'll figure this out," Uzair said, his voice steady. "We don't even know who that guy is. For all we know, he could just be a friend. But we need to find out for sure."

"How do we do that?" I asked, my voice shaky.

Uzair grinned, his eyes lighting up with a familiar spark of determination. "Simple—we follow the trail. You said you saw her coming out of that shop, right? Tomorrow, we start there. We ask around, maybe talk to some of the shopkeepers, see if anyone knows her or that guy. London's big, but people talk. If they're regulars, someone will know something."

I nodded, feeling a mix of hope and uncertainty. It wasn't much of a plan, but it was something. Uzair's confidence gave me a sliver of strength to hold on to.

The next morning, we set out early, retracing my steps to the shop where I had seen Lily. I felt nervous, like my entire life hung in the balance of what we might find. We walked into the shop—a small, cozy cafe tucked in the corner of the street. It had an old-world charm, with wooden beams and warm lighting.

Uzair took the lead, casually chatting with the barista while I stood awkwardly by the counter, scanning the room for any sign of Lily. After a few minutes, Uzair returned, a smirk on his face.

"The guy working here remembers her. He said she comes in every week, usually with that same guy. He's seen them a few times. But get this—they're not a couple. Just friends, apparently. He said they chat and laugh, but nothing romantic."

I felt a rush of relief and confusion all at once. "Just friends? Are you sure?"

Uzair nodded. "Yeah, seems like it. We can try talking to some other places, but it's starting to sound like this guy is just a normal friend, not someone she's involved with."

The weight on my chest eased a little, though it didn't disappear entirely. I still had no idea what Lily's life looked like now, and seeing her with someone else—even if they were just friends— stirred up so many emotions. But at least now I knew that all wasn't lost. There was still a chance, no matter how small.

As we left the cafe, Uzair clapped me on the back. "See, man? It's not as bad as you thought. Now we just have to figure out what you're going to say when you finally see her."

The thought of that moment terrified me. But for now, at least, we had a path forward. We would keep digging, find out more, and maybe—just maybe—I would get the chance to make things right.

As we stood there in the cafe, chatting with the barista, the door opened, and I heard Uzair gasp softly beside me. "Lily?" he called out, his voice filled with surprise. I turned, my heart skipping a beat.

There she was.

Lily stood in the doorway, her eyes wide with shock, then lighting up as she saw Uzair. "Uzair!" she exclaimed, rushing toward him with a laugh. She hugged him tightly, like they were picking up from where they left off, as if the years hadn't created the distance between them. The warmth between them was undeniable, and I could see the joy in her face as she clung to him, like two old friends who had been through too much and yet not enough.

"Wow, Uzair, you look... so different!" Lily said, pulling back with a playful smile, her eyes sparkling. "Everything about you—look at you! I can't believe it's really you."

Uzair chuckled, rubbing the back of his head awkwardly. "I could say the same about you, Lil. It's been forever."

As they exchanged words, Uzair moved slightly to the side, and that's when her eyes landed on me. For a split second, the world seemed to stop.

Our eyes met.

It was like time froze between us, a thousand unspoken words hanging in the air. She stared at me, and I could see so many emotions flickering across her face—surprise, pain, confusion, maybe even a touch of that old love buried deep beneath the surface. My heart ached as I looked at her, the memories flooding back. It was all there—every unsaid word, every missed moment, every chance I never took.

But just as quickly, something shifted in her expression. The vulnerability faded, replaced by a steely resolve. She turned her gaze away, almost like she couldn't bear to look at me any longer. And just like that, the connection snapped.

"Anyway, Uzair," she said, her voice steady but distant, ignoring my presence as if I wasn't standing right there, "tell me everything! What brings you here?"

My heart dropped as I realized what was happening. She wasn't going to acknowledge me. The years, the silence, everything between us—it was too much. She was pretending I wasn't there, and in that moment, I didn't have the strength to speak up. I stood there, feeling small, feeling lost, feeling like I had missed my chance.

Uzair shot me a glance, his brow furrowing in concern, but he didn't push it. He turned back to Lily, trying to keep the conversation light, but I couldn't hear them anymore. The pain in my chest was too much. I needed to get out of there.

I quietly slipped away, my footsteps heavy as I left the cafe. I didn't say a word. I just walked, letting the cold air hit my face, trying to make sense of what had just happened. How had everything gone so wrong? How had we ended up like this—strangers, pretending not to see each other, pretending the past didn't exist?

By the time I reached my place, I felt numb. I didn't want to feel anything anymore. But no matter how hard I tried, the image of Lily's face, the coldness in her eyes, was burned into my mind.

I had lost her. And it felt like I had lost a piece of myself too.

I reached home, my mind swirling in a chaotic mix of emotions. The door clicked shut behind me, but it felt like the world had just opened up into a void. I leaned against the cool wall, staring into the dimly lit room, unsure of what to think or feel.

What just happened back at the cafe? My heart raced at the memory of Lily, her laughter filling the air just moments before she turned away from me. I felt an ache in my chest, a hollow reminder of everything we once shared, now overshadowed by the distance that had grown between us. How could I let things spiral so far out of control?

I wandered into the living room, running my fingers over the furniture like it was foreign to me. The familiar surroundings felt strangely alien, echoing with the silence of my solitude. I sank onto the couch, my thoughts racing. When would Uzair come back? What would he say? Did he even have answers to the questions swirling in my mind?

Every minute felt like an eternity. I replayed the moment in the cafe over and over, analyzing every word, every glance, every smile. My heart fluttered at the thought of Lily, yet sank at the realization that she seemed so different now. She had moved on, and I was still stuck in the past, tangled in a web of what-ifs and regrets.

Finally, the front door creaked open, and Uzair stepped in, looking a bit worn but with a glimmer of hope in his eyes. "Nile!" he called out, the sound snapping me from my thoughts.

I sat up, my heart racing again, a rush of anticipation mixed with anxiety. "What happened?" I asked, my voice almost a whisper.

Uzair kicked off his shoes and walked over, his expression serious. "You're not going to believe this, but I think we're on to something." He pulled out his phone, scrolling through the messages he'd exchanged while we were at the cafe. "I spoke to the barista. He mentioned that Lily was planning to meet up with some old friends this weekend. He didn't know exactly who, but it's a start."

Hope flickered within me, battling the shadows of despair. "Do you think she'll be there? With him?" I tried to keep my voice steady, but the uncertainty gnawed at me.

Uzair shrugged, leaning back against the wall. "I don't know, man. But we have to find out. We can't just give up now. You've got to talk to her. Clear the air."

I nodded, my heart pounding in my chest. It was a chance—a chance to confront everything I had been avoiding. But as I looked at Uzair, I felt the weight of the moment pressing down on me. Would I even know what to say?

"Thanks for pushing me, Uzair," I said, my voice filled with gratitude. "I know I messed up. But I don't want to let her slip away again. I need to find out what's really going on."

Uzair smiled, clapping me on the shoulder. "That's the spirit. Just remember, whatever happens, you're not alone in this."

And as I sat there, surrounded by the familiar comfort of friendship, I felt a glimmer of hope. Maybe, just maybe, I could find my way back to Lily.

Days turned into a blur as Lily continued to avoid me. It was like I was stuck in a never-ending loop of awkward encounters and missed opportunities. I'd catch glimpses of her around campus—laughing with friends, deep in conversation—but every time I tried to approach her, she'd slip away like a ghost, leaving me standing there with nothing but my racing heart and an empty smile.

I tried to play it cool. After all, I was a successful businessman now, right? But every time I thought of a clever way to break the ice, it felt like I was diving headfirst into an ice-cold pool. One day, I even resorted to asking Uzair for help, but his ideas were about as helpful as a chocolate teapot.

"Why don't you send her a funny meme?" he suggested. "You know, something relatable about friendship and all that."

So, I scoured the internet for the perfect meme. I found a picture of a cat looking utterly bewildered, with the caption, "When you see your best friend ignoring you, but you still love them anyway."

I nervously sent it her way, waiting for the response. Nothing. Crickets. It felt like I'd thrown a message in a bottle into the ocean, and now I was just staring at the waves, hoping it would somehow find its way back.

Another day, I decided to take a more direct approach. I overheard her talking about a coffee shop she loved. I thought about casually showing up there, ordering my usual, and somehow, we'd end up in the same conversation. But as I entered the cafe, I tripped over my own feet and sent my coffee flying, landing right on the table where she sat with her friends. Smooth, right?

"Hey, Nile! Clumsy as ever, huh?" one of her friends laughed, while Lily just stared at her coffee soaked table, a mix of sympathy and disbelief on her face.

I laughed awkwardly, wiping at the table with a napkin, but the moment felt completely lost. Lily was nice enough to help me clean up, but when I looked into her eyes, I could feel the wall she had built between us. It was frustrating!

One night, I even considered going full-on romantic comedy. I bought a bouquet of flowers and planned to surprise her. I envisioned her eyes lighting up, the joy of rekindling our friendship. But when I arrived at her dorm, my hands full of blooms, I found her door closed, a sign hung up reading "Do Not Disturb."

"Perfect," I muttered to myself. Instead of leaving the flowers outside, I took a deep breath and knocked. I waited, holding the flowers like they were the last slice of pizza at a party.

"Go away!" Lily's muffled voice called from inside.

Deflated, I turned to leave, mumbling to myself about how ridiculous I must look. But then I had a sudden thought. "What if I just leave them here?"

So, I awkwardly set the flowers down outside her door, giving it one last hopeful knock. "These are for you! Whenever you're ready!" I called out before walking away, feeling slightly better but still a bit foolish.

Despite all my failed attempts, I couldn't shake the hope that maybe one day, she'd let me in again. But for now, I was left with my clumsy antics and a determination to find a way to break through her walls—no matter how many funny mishaps it took.

As the days passed and Lily continued to avoid me, Uzair became my comedic sidekick in this tragicomedy of errors. He had taken it upon himself to help me win her back, but his methods were... well, let's just say they were wildly unconventional.

One afternoon, as we sat in our dorm room, I sighed heavily. "I just don't know what to do, Uzair. Every time I see her, I freeze up like a deer caught in headlights."

Uzair, who was sprawled on the bed scrolling through his phone, suddenly perked up. "What if we create a distraction? Something so ridiculous that it'll make her laugh and break the ice!"

I raised an eyebrow, intrigued but skeptical. "And how do you propose we do that?"

"Simple! A flash mob!" he exclaimed, as if he had just solved a complex equation. "We'll gather everyone in the cafeteria at lunch, and when she walks in, we'll start dancing!"

I burst out laughing. "You want me to dance? I have two left feet!"

"Exactly! It'll be hilarious!" he replied, already typing messages to our friends in a group chat.

I shook my head, trying to stifle my laughter. "You're crazy."

But before I knew it, we were gathering our friends in secret. The plan was set, and soon I found myself standing awkwardly in the cafeteria with a group of our friends, all trying to act casual while hiding our excitement.

Lily walked in, and the moment she did, we sprang into action. The music blasted through the speakers, and we launched into a series of clumsy dance moves that had absolutely no rhythm. I flailed my arms and tried to follow Uzair's lead, but I ended up tripping over my own feet and nearly toppling over a table.

The entire cafeteria erupted in laughter, and even Lily couldn't help but smile, a spark of recognition crossing her face. But just as I thought we might have broken the ice, she turned to leave, shaking her head with an amused expression.

"Wait! We're not done!" Uzair shouted, pulling me along as we chased after her, still dancing awkwardly.

After that failed flash mob, I decided to take a different approach. One evening, I confided in Uzair about my latest plan. "I'm thinking of getting her a cute stuffed animal. Something light- hearted. You know, like a peace offering?"

Uzair's eyes lit up with mischief. "Why not take it a step further? Let's stuff it with a recording of you singing a love song!"

"Absolutely not!" I exclaimed, horrified at the thought. "I can't sing!"

"Exactly! That's the charm!" Uzair insisted, laughing so hard he nearly fell off his chair.

I rolled my eyes, but the idea stuck with me. "Fine, I'll get the stuffed animal, but no singing!"

The next day, I marched into a local store and found the cutest little bear, dressed in a tiny hoodie that read, "Hug Me!" I could already picture Lily's smile when she saw it. But, of course, I needed Uzair's help for the delivery.

"Here's the plan," Uzair said, grinning from ear to ear. "We'll have a 'surprise bear delivery' at the library, and I'll pretend to be a courier."

"Are you sure about this?" I asked, already imagining how this could go wrong.

"Trust me! It'll be legendary!" he assured me.

So, on the designated day, we waited outside the library. Uzair put on a fake mustache and sunglasses, trying to look like an undercover agent. When Lily walked in, he stepped forward dramatically, holding the bear aloft.

"Delivery for Miss Lily!" he declared in a faux-serious tone.

Lily stopped and blinked in confusion, a smile creeping onto her face despite herself. "What is this?"

"Your special delivery from the 'Nile Express,'" Uzair announced, trying to suppress laughter.

I stepped forward, my heart racing. "Uh, yeah! I thought you might like this." I handed her the bear, my palms sweaty.

Lily looked from the bear to me, and I held my breath, waiting for her reaction. She burst out laughing, the sound music to my ears. "This is adorable, but what's with the delivery?"

"Just a friendly gesture!" I said, trying to sound casual while Uzair was practically cracking up behind me.

Lily's laughter faded, and she looked at me with an emotion I hadn't seen in a while. "Thanks, Nile. Really. This means a lot."

I felt a flicker of hope as she hugged the bear tightly, and for the first time in weeks, it felt like we were on the path to mending what had been broken. Thanks to Uzair's ridiculous antics, I had managed to get a real smile from her. Maybe there was still a chance for us after all.

That night, Uzair and I were sitting on the rooftop of our rented apartment, the cool breeze sweeping over us. The sky was scattered with stars, and the faint hum of the city was all around. We hadn't said much for the past few minutes, just smoking and staring off into the distance. Then Uzair broke the silence.

"Nile," he began, glancing at me with that thoughtful expression he always had when he wanted to say something serious. "We're leaving in five days. That's all we have left here."

I took a long drag from my cigarette, exhaled slowly, and stared at the night sky, letting his words sink in. I knew what was coming.

"You've been waiting all these years, carrying this weight. Don't you think it's time to let it go? If you leave without talking to Lily, it'll haunt you forever," he said, his voice calm but insistent.

I let out a tired sigh, flicking the ash off the cigarette. "What if it's too late, Uzair? What if she doesn't care anymore? What if… she doesn't even want to hear it?" My voice cracked slightly, betraying the emotion I'd tried to keep buried.

Uzair leaned forward, resting his arms on his knees. "Listen, man," he said softly. "It's not about what happens next—it's about you being at peace. Carrying guilt like this will eat you alive. You need to say sorry, not just for her, but for yourself too. Otherwise…" He trailed off, knowing I understood what he meant.

The thought of those five days felt like a ticking clock in my chest. I knew I couldn't run from this forever. Every time I saw Lily, every second she avoided me, it chipped away at me from the inside. Uzair was right. If I left London without saying sorry, I'd be stuck in the same loop of regret for the rest of my life.

I nodded slowly, though it felt like a mountain was sitting on my shoulders. "You think I have a chance?" I asked quietly.

Uzair smiled. "Nile, it's not about a chance. It's about being brave enough to face what's in front of you."

The silence between us was thick with emotion, and the weight of unspoken memories sat heavily on my chest. I knew what I had to do, but that didn't make it any easier. Five days. Five days to find closure, or risk losing it forever.

I put out my cigarette, watching the glow of the ember fade. "Alright," I whispered, more to myself than to him. "I'll tell her."

Uzair gave me a reassuring nod, as if to say, *I've got your back, no matter what.* And for the first time in a long while, I felt the smallest sliver of hope start to creep in.

This wasn't just about finding forgiveness—it was about re-claiming the part of me I had lost along the way.

The clock was ticking. Five days. And I wasn't going to let them slip away.

The next morning, I woke up with a heavy heart and a racing mind. The sun filtered through the thin curtains, painting golden streaks across the room. For a moment, I just lay there, staring at the ceiling, my mind tangled in thoughts. Today was the day. There was no more running, no more hiding—I had to face Lily.

I sat up, rubbing my face as if I could scrub away the weight of the years. Every heartbeat echoed with anxiety. The memories, the regrets, the words I should've said back then—they all swirled around me like a storm. I knew that today would either break me or set me free. But I couldn't carry this burden any longer. I had to tell her.

I stood up, glancing around the room. Uzair was still asleep, sprawled across the bed with one leg hanging off the side. I smiled a little at the sight. He looked so peaceful, like we weren't on the edge of a moment that could change everything.

I walked over to the window and looked outside. London was waking up—people on their way to work, shops unlocking their doors, the streets slowly coming to life. But for me, the world felt smaller, as if it revolved around just one thing—Lily.

Taking a deep breath, I forced myself to start the day. I brushed my teeth, splashed water on my face, and stared into the mirror. "You've got this," I whispered to myself, trying to convince the reflection. But the reflection just looked back, uncertain and afraid.

I threw on a simple black t-shirt and a jacket, my hands trembling slightly as I zipped it up. The thought of seeing her, of standing in front of her and trying to apologize for all the years and mistakes—it was enough to make me want to turn back. But Uzair's words from last night echoed in my mind:

"It's not about a chance. It's about being brave enough to face what's in front of you."

I looked at Uzair again. He was still fast asleep, his soft snores filling the quiet room. For a moment, I considered waking him. But I knew this was a battle I had to fight on my own.

With one last glance at the mirror, I whispered, "It's time." And with that, I took a deep breath and stepped out of the room, ready to face the day—and Lily— no matter what lay ahead.

When I reached the shop, I saw Lily outside, carefully placing things in their spots, one by one. The early morning light kissed her face, her every movement delicate yet determined. But something gnawed at me. I couldn't shake the thought—*Why was she still doing all of this?* She came from a wealthy family, a world far removed from the small struggles of running a shop. Yet here she was, tending to every detail herself. It didn't make sense, but I let the thought drift away. I had more important things on my mind.

As I moved closer, I saw her struggling with a heavy box. She shifted it, her arms trembling under the weight. Before I could even think, I stepped in, grabbing the other side just in time. My hand brushed against hers—soft and familiar, sending a warmth through me like a spark igniting from deep within. For a second, it felt like time paused.

Her scent, the light breeze that carried her familiar essence, the warmth of her skin—it all crashed over me, stirring memories I had buried deep. My heart thudded in my chest. *There she was—the girl I once never saw clearly, the love I foolishly ignored.*

She exhaled sharply, her eyes narrowing as she pushed the box down onto the ground. She straightened up, brushing her hands off with a curt, "Thank you," cold and distant.

Before I could respond, she turned to leave, her expression guarded and unreadable, as if she had built walls around herself—walls I had helped construct.

"Lily, wait!" I said, reaching out and gently grasping her wrist. Her skin felt warm beneath my fingers, but it was the chill in her eyes that sent a shiver through me.

She tried to pull away, but I held on, softly—just enough to stop her. "Please, listen to me. I know I was wrong. I know I hurt you, and I can't tell you how sorry I am."

Her expression didn't change, but I kept going. Words poured out of me—words that had been locked away for far too long.

"I was young, Lily. I was immature and selfish, lost in my own world. I thought I knew everything, but I didn't know a damn thing about love… or about you. I was so obsessed with chasing after Lucy, chasing after something that was never real. And in doing that, I destroyed the one thing that mattered most—you."

Her lips pressed into a tight line, but I caught the flicker of something in her eyes—hurt, maybe? Or was it something more?

"I know now, Lily. I know you loved me. And I was too blind to see it. Too stupid to realize what I had right in front of me. I hurt you in ways I can't undo, and I hate myself for that. Every day, I've lived with the regret, knowing I lost the one person who cared about me more than anyone else."

My voice cracked, and I felt my chest tighten. But I kept going, desperate to make her understand.

"Please, Lily. I can't go back and fix the past, but I can promise you this—I won't hurt you again. I need you in my life. Please, give me one more chance. I know I don't deserve it, but I'll do anything to make it right."

The silence between us was unbearable, thick with unspoken pain and lingering hope. I searched her face for any sign that she might still care, that she might forgive me.

Her lips trembled slightly, as if she wanted to say something, but she held back. And then—just for a moment—her eyes softened.

She froze for a moment, her breath uneven, and I could see something flicker in her eyes—pain, anger, or maybe memories she didn't want to revisit. But then, just as quickly, her face hardened into a mask of indifference, and her tone cut through me like a cold blade.

"Hey, listen," she snapped, her voice sharp and guarded. "I don't know what you're talking about, okay? I didn't love you. Whatever you think—just... forget it. I already have. It's all in the past now, and honestly, you should do the same."

Her words hit me harder than I expected. I could feel my chest tighten as if the air had been sucked out of my lungs. I stood there, stunned, replaying her words over and over in my head, trying to convince myself she didn't mean them. That this was just her way of keeping the pain at bay. But the way she looked at me—detached, almost empty—it was like she had built a fortress around herself, one I might never be able to break through.

"You... forgot everything?" I whispered, my voice hoarse and brittle, as if speaking louder would make it all too real.

"Yeah," she said, with a short, bitter laugh that stung more than anything else. "So, if you came here thinking we'd have some big emotional moment where everything gets fixed, let me save you the trouble—it's not happening. You should just leave."

Her words were like nails driving deeper into the cracks of my heart. I searched her eyes for anything—*anything*—that could tell me this wasn't how she truly felt. That maybe, buried somewhere under all that bitterness, the Lily I knew still existed. The girl who used to laugh with me, who held onto hope, who made me believe in things I didn't understand back then.

But all I saw was a wall I had built myself—brick by brick, mistake by mistake. And now, I stood on the other side of it, helpless to tear it down.

She turned away, adjusting the things on the shop counter, as if dismissing me like I was just another customer she needed to send on his way.

"Lily, wait... Please..." I whispered, but the words felt small, insignificant in the face of everything I had done wrong.

She didn't wait. Didn't even flinch. Just like that, she went back to her world, and I was left standing there—crushed under the weight of my regrets.

The part that hurt the most wasn't even her words. It was the fact that they could be true. *What if she really had moved on?*

What if, after all this time, I was the only one still holding on? And she… she had learned to live without me.

I felt something heavy settle in my chest—an ache that made it hard to breathe. I wanted to scream, cry, anything to release the storm building inside me, but all I could do was stand there, paralyzed by the harsh reality she had handed me.

And in that moment, I knew: this wasn't going to be easy. If I wanted to fix things, if I wanted even the slightest chance at redemption, it wouldn't come with a single apology. It would take more than words.

But the worst part? I wasn't sure if I could even try. Because how do you fight for someone who tells you they've already let go?

I dragged myself home, feeling like life had lost all meaning. Everything felt hollow, like the air around me had turned heavy and suffocating. The weight of Lily's words settled deep into my chest, draining me of every ounce of hope I had left. What was the point of anything now? It felt like every step I took led nowhere, and the future was nothing but a blur I didn't care to walk into.

When I reached the apartment, Uzair was sitting at the kitchen table, casually munching on toast, his headphones dangling around his neck. As if nothing in the world had gone wrong, he looked up, grinning like he always did.

"Hey you! Where were you, sleepyhead?" Uzair called out cheerfully. "Come on, breakfast's waiting.

Let's fill that belly."

I sat down across from him, silent, staring blankly at the plate he pushed toward me. The eggs, the toast—it was all just food, but it felt like it didn't belong to me. Nothing did. Uzair's lightheartedness was a stark contrast to the storm raging inside me. I wanted to respond, to say anything, but the words just wouldn't come.

Uzair noticed the silence lingering too long, so in his usual way, he tried to lighten the mood. "Come on, man. You ready now?" He shot me a playful smirk. "Four days left! Let's make the most of it, huh? We'll go crazy. Maybe find someone new, huh? Forget all this drama."

The entire day, I couldn't sit still. I kept checking the time every few minutes, pacing back and forth across the room, my heart racing with anticipation. I rearranged the table at least five times, making sure everything looked perfect. Every small noise made me jump, thinking it might be her. I stood by the mirror, fixing my hair for the hundredth time, hoping to look better than I felt.

Uzair noticed my nervous energy and leaned against the wall with his signature grin.

"Bro, you've already combed your hair more times today than you did the whole year we spent together. Relax! She's not coming to interview you."

I shot him a glare. "Man, this isn't funny, Uzair. What if I mess it up?"

Uzair laughed. "If you mess it up? You've *been* messing it up since the day you met her. But hey, if she hasn't killed you yet, I'd say you're safe tonight." He winked and patted me on the back. "Come on, champ. Just don't say anything stupid, and you'll be fine."

I shook my head, trying to calm my nerves. "Easy for you to say."

Uzair smirked. "Oh yeah? You should've seen yourself just now—practically *flirting* with the cutlery. If you bring this energy to Lily, you'll have her marrying the forks and spoons."

"Shut up, Uzair," I mumbled, though I couldn't help but crack a small smile.

Just then, there was a knock at the door, and every muscle in my body tensed. My heart felt like it was going to explode.

"Well, good luck, Romeo." Uzair chuckled as he pushed me toward the door. "And for the love of God, please don't embarrass us both."

Taking a deep breath, I reached for the handle, my hand trembling slightly. As the door swung open, it felt like the air was sucked out of the room.

There she was—Lily. But standing next to her, hand in hand, was the same guy we had seen with her at the shop that day. My heart sank like a stone thrown into deep water. Even Uzair, standing behind me, went silent. His usual grin disappeared, replaced by a look of disbelief.

Without saying a word, I turned away and left the room, my chest tight and my throat burning. I could hear Uzair calling my name, but I didn't stop. I just needed to get away—away from her, from them, from everything.

I found myself on the rooftop, the night sky above me cold and indifferent. The cigarette in my hand shook as I lit it, inhaling deeply to calm the storm raging inside me. But it didn't help. Nothing could help.

I exhaled slowly, watching the smoke curl up into the darkness. And then the words slipped out of my mouth, barely more than a whisper.

"Accept it, Nile… She's gone. She's really gone."

I leaned against the railing, the weight of those words crushing me. My chest felt like it was caving in. The tears started flowing, and no matter how hard I tried to stop them, they kept coming. The cigarette fell from my hand, forgotten, as the sobs wracked my body.

It wasn't just the thought of Lily being with someone else—it was everything. All the missed chances, the unspoken words, the times I could've fought for her but didn't.

Tears blurred my vision as I stared into the night, lost in my regrets. It was like all the pain I had buried for so long came rushing to the surface, drowning me. I didn't know what to do or where to go from here.

And for the first time in a long time, I felt truly, hopelessly lost. After what felt like an eternity, I finally saw the car pull away, taking Lily and that guy with it. A wave of despair crashed over me as I stood there, the cigarette hanging limply from my fingers. I couldn't believe it. I was losing her, and there was

nothing I could do about it.

I took a long drag from the cigarette, trying to drown my sorrow in smoke. The world around me blurred as I fought to hold back the tears that threatened to spill over. I was leaving tomorrow, and I couldn't shake the feeling that it would be forever.

"Okay, I'm done," I muttered to myself, anger bubbling up inside me. "I'm just going to pack and go."

But deep down, I knew it wasn't that simple. I felt broken, utterly shattered. All the moments we shared—the laughter, the whispered secrets, the dreams for the future—flooded my mind. Each memory pierced my heart like shards of glass. I couldn't help it; the tears began to fall, and I let out a choked sob, feeling completely alone in my grief.

As I turned to leave, Uzair stepped forward, his face a mix of concern and frustration. "Shut up, Nile. Just stop!"

But before I could respond, I heard a voice that sent chills down my spine. "Let him speak."

I froze, turning slowly to see Lily standing there, her expression unreadable. The moonlight caught her features, illuminating the pain etched on her face. It felt surreal—like I was seeing a ghost.

"I... I didn't expect to see you here," I stammered, my heart racing. I felt vulnerable, exposed, like she could see straight through the walls I had built around my heart.

"You don't have to pretend around me," she said softly, her voice a whisper in the night. "You can be honest, Nile."

Honest? How could I be honest when all I felt was a storm of emotions? I opened my mouth to say something, but the words caught in my throat. I wanted to shout, to express all the hurt I felt, but instead, all that came out was a strangled cry.

"I'm broken, Lily. I don't even know how to fix this," I admitted, my voice shaking. "You… you were my everything, and now you're just… gone."

I could feel the tears streaming down my face, unbidden. I was powerless to stop them. My heart felt like it was being crushed under the weight of regret and despair.

For a moment, all I could hear was my ragged breathing, the sound of the night around us. And then I noticed Uzair's eyes darting between us, uncertain. He looked torn, wanting to intervene but knowing this was something I had to face myself.

Lily stepped closer, her expression softening as she met my gaze. "I didn't mean to hurt you," she said, her voice breaking.

"But things have changed, Nile. I don't know how to explain it."

"Then tell me," I pleaded, my heart pounding in my chest. "Tell me why you chose him. Why didn't you fight for us?"

Her silence spoke volumes. The air between us thickened with unspoken words and unresolved feelings.

"I've missed you every day," I confessed, the rawness of my emotions spilling out. "I can't just pretend like I don't care. You mean too much to me."

And in that moment, as I stood there trembling, exposed in my vulnerability, I felt the reality of my situation crash down around me. I was losing the only person who ever truly understood me, and the pain was unbearable.

I wiped my tears away furiously, unable to keep them at bay any longer. I felt small, like a child who had lost their way, and the ache in my chest was almost too much to bear.

Lily took a step closer, her eyes glistening with unshed tears. "Nile…"

But I couldn't hear her. All I felt was the emptiness threatening to consume me, and I turned away, desperate to escape the reality of it all. I stumbled back, feeling lost and defeated, hoping against hope that I could wake up from this nightmare.

In that dark moment, I realized something—life without her would be unbearable, but I didn't know how to fix what was broken between us. All I could do was cry and hope she would understand

I picked at my food, dragging the fork across the plate without any real intention of eating. "Uzair…" I muttered quietly, looking at him with heaviness in my gaze. "I think we should leave now. There's no point staying any longer."

The words came out flat, devoid of the fire or energy Uzair was trying to spark in me. My voice felt distant, like it didn't belong to me. "I just… I can't do this anymore. There's no reason to stay. Let's just go back and… I don't know. Just go back."

Uzair's smile faded, his playful demeanor slipping for just a moment. He knew me well enough to sense how deeply I was hurting, but he didn't say anything. He just nodded a quiet acceptance that this wasn't the time to push me.

"Okay," he whispered, as if understanding the unspoken weight in my words. "We'll do whatever you want, Nile."

I pushed my chair back, leaving the half-eaten breakfast on the table. The exhaustion—both emotional and physical—pulled me like gravity. "I'll be in my room," I mumbled.

Without waiting for a response, I walked to my room and shut the door behind me. The silence that greeted me was deafening, amplifying the ache in my chest. I collapsed onto the bed, staring blankly at the ceiling, as memories of Lily swirled in my mind like a haunting melody that wouldn't stop playing.

Sleep pulled me under soon enough, but even in sleep, I found no peace. Dreams of her eyes, her laughter, and her rejection played on a loop, tormenting me in ways that reality already had. And so, I slept for the whole day—hoping, maybe, that when I woke up, everything would feel different. But deep down, I knew it wouldn't.

The next day started like any other, with Uzair moving through his usual routine, assuming I was just out for a walk. But as the hours stretched into afternoon, a knot of worry began to tighten in his chest. I was nowhere to be found. Uzair had checked the apartment, called my phone—no response. At first, he thought I needed space, but by now, it didn't feel right.

His concern grew, and Uzair decided to search for me. He wandered through the streets, revisiting places he knew I might go—the park, the coffee shop, even some of the corners we had explored together over the past few days. But I was nowhere.

As frustration began to settle in, Uzair knew there was one last place he had to check. He hurried to Lily's shop, arriving just as she was closing for the day. She was locking the door, unaware of the storm brewing within Uzair's mind.

"Lily!" Uzair called out, slightly breathless.

She turned toward him, confused. "What's wrong, Uzair?"

"Nile... he's missing. I've searched everywhere, but I can't find him. Do you know where he could be?" Uzair's worry was now palpable, and the moment Lily saw it, her expression changed from mild annoyance to concern.

Without hesitation, she said, "Let's go find him."

They scoured the streets together, checking places Nile had frequented in the past. Every corner of the city felt like a dead end. After hours of searching, both were exhausted, but Uzair refused to give up. Then, by sheer luck, a group of children playing nearby caught their attention.

"Hey, misters," one of the kids said, "are you looking for someone? We saw a guy wandering by the old forest... kinda looked lost."

Uzair and Lily exchanged worried glances. "A forest?" Lily asked.

The kid pointed toward a patch of dense trees at the edge of the neighborhood. "Yeah, he went that way."

They made their way toward the forest, fear settling into their bones with every step. The air was thick, the kind that made everything feel heavier. It wasn't exactly a jungle, but the dense trees and overgrown paths gave it a wild, disorienting feel.

At last, they spotted me—sitting on a weathered old bench, slouched over, looking completely drained of life. My shoulders were sagging, my clothes wrinkled, and my face etched with frustration and exhaustion. I was a shell of myself, lost in a void of emotions that I didn't know how to navigate.

"There he is," Lily whispered, her voice catching in her throat. For a brief second, she made a move to approach me, but Uzair gently grabbed her arm and stopped her.

"Wait," he said softly. "He's not okay. Let me talk to him first."

They slowly made their way toward me. In my haze, I noticed two figures moving closer, and as my blurry vision cleared, I saw her. Lily. The sight of her hit me like a punch to the chest, stirring everything I had buried deep within me.

But as soon as that hope flickered, it was snuffed out by the overwhelming exhaustion I felt. My body betrayed me, and my knees gave way, leaving me unable to stand. My heart wanted to reach for her, but my body was too weak to respond. It was like drowning in a dream where the shore was just within reach but still impossibly far.

I forced a smile, but it didn't even reach my eyes. I slumped forward, whispering, "Uzair... just take me home, man. Please. This city... it's killing me. I can't do this anymore. I need to leave."

Uzair knelt beside me, placing a hand on my back. "Okay, okay, bro," he whispered, his voice soft and steady. "You're not alone. We'll go back. Just rest for now. I've got you."

I felt Uzair's arm wrap around me as he helped me to my feet. My body felt like lead, but his steady support kept me from falling again. I gave one final glance toward Lily, hoping for something— anything—from her. But she remained quiet, standing a few steps away, her expression unreadable.

As Uzair guided me through the forest, I leaned on him, too exhausted to care about anything anymore. I had nothing left to say, nothing left to fight for—not now, at least. All I knew was that I wanted to leave. And for now, that was the only thing keeping me together.

Uzair led me home, walking slowly as I leaned on him. When we finally reached, he lit the small fireplace in our room, warming the space and me along with it. The flickering flames felt like a lifeline in the darkness I'd been drowning in. Uzair sat me down and, without a word, brought food to me, feeding me with his own hands. I was too drained to refuse.

"Here, bro. You need this more than you think," Uzair said with a half-smile, pressing a spoonful toward me. I ate in silence, but deep down, something in me softened. Uzair wasn't just a friend—he was a lifeline. The kind of friend who never let goes, even when you tried your best to slip away.

He always knew how to show up exactly when it mattered, in ways words couldn't. **A true champ**—the one person who never made me feel alone, no matter how lost I became. He didn't just support me; he carried my weight when I couldn't stand, laughed for me when I forgot how, and stayed when others left. And somehow, even in my brokenness, he never made me feel like a burden.

After eating, exhaustion overtook me. Uzair tucked a blanket around me, and the warmth lulled me into a deep sleep.

The next morning, life felt... lifeless. It was one of those day where everything felt numb—like I was just moving through the motions, breathing but not alive. The weight of my own mistakes sat heavy on my chest. I woke up hoping for clarity, but all I felt was emptiness.

I dragged myself out of bed and went to Uzair. "When are we leaving?" I asked quietly, trying to push through the fear of staying in a city that had brought nothing but heartbreak.

Uzair, sitting by the window with his coffee, looked over at me. "Not just yet," he said with a grin, setting the cup down. "Lily wants to have dinner with us tonight."

I froze. "What? What did you say?"

Uzair smiled, enjoying my stunned reaction. "You heard me. Lily wants dinner—*with us.* what do you think?"

I blinked, still struggling to process his words. After everything—after days of her avoiding me, shutting me out— now she wanted dinner? I didn't know whether to believe it. I stared at Uzair like he was joking, but he wasn't.

"You're serious?" I whispered.

"Dead serious." Uzair gave me a playful nudge. "So... you in or what?"

I nodded slowly, almost in disbelief. "Yeah… yeah, okay. I'm in."

A strange, nervous excitement began to build in me—like hope, fragile and trembling. I couldn't explain it, but just knowing that Lily wanted to meet us gave me something I hadn't felt in a long time. I wasn't going to mess this up. I *couldn't* mess this up.

I spent the entire day preparing for the dinner. I cooked everything by myself—every dish, every little detail. I wanted it to be perfect, not just for her but for myself too. It felt good, focusing on something meaningful, something with the potential to change everything.

For the first time in what felt like forever, I was happy. There was warmth in my chest, like a spark of hope I hadn't felt since the day I saw her again. Maybe this was a chance to fix things. Maybe this time, things would be different.

And as I set the last plate on the table, I took a deep breath, looking around at the small dinner I had prepared. It wasn't grand, but it was mine. And for the first time in a long while, I smiled.

The moment I heard the car, I knew it was them—Lily and that guy. I stood still in the darkness, watching as they left. My chest tightened. My mind screamed, *This is it—she's really gone.* When the car disappeared into the night, I forced my heavy legs to carry me downstairs.

Uzair was sitting at the table, the food untouched. I stared at the plates, the untouched meal mocking my hopes. My chest felt hollow, my throat burning as if I had swallowed hot coals. I sat across from Uzair, my eyes stinging as I whispered, "Uzi… I can't stay here. I just can't. She loves someone else."

My voice cracked as I continued, "What's the point of being here? I thought maybe… just maybe there was still something left between us. But there isn't, man. I lost her… I lost her a long time ago." My head dropped into my hands, and before I could stop it, the tears began to flow. Hot, heavy tears, years of regret and heartbreak spilling out at once.

Uzair scooted closer, reaching out to me. "Nile, stop it, please. It's not what you think—just slow down."

But I shook my head, ignoring him. The words kept pouring out, raw and broken. "I thought I could fix it, Uzair. I thought I could say sorry, and maybe she'd see me again—really see me, like she used to. But she's moved on… She's with someone else now. What am I even doing here?" I could barely breathe through the sobs that took over. "I'm leaving, Uzi. I'm leaving right now. I can't stay here another second."

I stood up abruptly, wiping my face on my sleeve. My legs trembled, and my vision blurred with tears, but I didn't care. Uzair jumped up, grabbing my arm. "Nile, listen to me! You're not thinking straight—just stop for a second, man."

But in that moment, I couldn't hear him. I pulled my arm free, stumbling toward the door. My heart was shattered, and every step felt heavier with the weight of my mistakes.

Just as Uzair tried to stop me again, a voice, soft and certain, cut through the room.

"Let him go, Uzair."

I froze in place, the sound of her voice like a jolt through my system. My pulse pounded in my ears. Slowly, I turned to see her standing there. Lily. She was still here. She hadn't left with him.

My breath hitched. She had stayed.

She had stayed the night.

As she came closer, her eyes were shining with unshed tears. There was a trembling in her voice, each word like a dagger, cutting through the silence between us.

"Was this it, Nile? Just seeing me with another guy, and you couldn't handle it? How do you think I handled it when you gave all your love to someone else—someone who never even cared about you the way I did?"

Her voice cracked, and she wiped at her eyes, but the tears kept coming.

"You know what hurts, Nile? It's not even that you didn't love me back… It's that you ignored me. I never asked you to love me, but you didn't even give me a chance to love you in my way.

I just… I

wanted to be there for you. But you shut me out."

She sank onto the bench beside me, her shoulders trembling under the weight of everything she had held in for years. "The day you left… That didn't break me. But the slap—" She paused, her voice faltering. "That broke me, Nile. It shattered everything between us. You left me standing there, and I told myself you'd come back, even if just to check on me. But you never did."

Her voice grew softer, filled with years of hurt and abandonment. "You knew what Kevin meant to Mom. After he died, she believed you'd take his place. You were supposed to be the one to step in. But you didn't. You left—just like Dad. And I stayed here, lost. I spent days crawling through the filth, trying to survive, wishing for someone to tell me I wasn't alone. But no one came. Not even you."

She leaned in closer now, her breath shaky, the words heavy with anger, love, and unbearable sadness. "I told myself I hated you, Nile. I told myself every single day that I hated you. I

wanted to hate you... because it hurt less than loving someone who abandoned me."

Lily took a step closer, and the weight of years reflected in her tear-filled eyes. Her voice, low and trembling, slipped through the silence like a whisper made of broken glass. "Nile, I was alive... but I was dying. Dying in the darkness of a love you never saw. Every day, I was suffocating, waiting for you. But you never came."

Her words left me breathless, guilt crashing over me like waves. I opened my mouth to speak, but no words would come.

She stood there, her chest rising and falling unevenly, holding back emotions she had locked away for far too long. And then, in a voice choked with anger and sorrow, she whispered:

"I hate you..."

She paused, her eyes squeezing shut as if saying it hurt more than holding it in.

"I hate you…"

A tear rolled down her cheek, and her body trembled as the final words broke through her sobs. "I hate you, Nile…"

And then, before I could react, she threw her arms around me, clinging to me with all her strength, as if letting go would tear her apart. Her face pressed into my shoulder, and the hatred in her words melted into a desperate confession.

"But I love you… I love you so much."

I stood frozen, her embrace burning through every layer of guilt, regret, and shame that had weighed me down for years. Her sobs wracked her small frame, and with each breath, I could feel the depth of her pain—a pain I had caused, knowingly and unknowingly.

"I'm sorry," I whispered, my voice cracking under the weight of emotions. I hugged her tighter, afraid that if I let go, I'd lose her forever. "I was so blind, Lily… I didn't see it. I didn't see you."

Her tears soaked through my shirt, and I pressed my face into her hair, holding her like she was the only thing keeping me from falling apart. "I was a fool… lost in my own world, chasing something that was never real. And I hurt you—again and again. I abandoned you when you needed me the most."

Her arms tightened around me, her sobs soft but relentless, as if the years of silence were finally unraveling. "You didn't just hurt me, Nile…" she whispered. "You *left* me."

I pulled her even closer, feeling the weight of those words cut through me. "I know. And I'll never forgive myself for that. But please, Lily… let me make it right now. Just give me a chance to love you the way you deserved all along."

She didn't answer with words. She just held me tighter, as if trying to bind all the broken pieces together. And in that moment, it didn't matter how much time had been lost, how many mistakes had been made. All that mattered was that we were here—together, in each other's arms, finally allowing ourselves to feel everything.

It was raw. It was painful. But it was real.

And for the first time in years, I felt like I had found home again.

Her embrace crushed me in ways words never could. I stood there, frozen, as every wall I had built around my heart came crashing down. I felt her tears against my neck, her fragile body trembling with the weight of her emotions—and something inside me shattered too.

I wrapped my arms around her, holding her tighter, as if by doing so, I could take back all the years of pain I had caused. In that moment, no words could fix it, no apology was big enough. We stood there, two broken souls wrapped in each other's arms, in the quiet of the night. And in that moment, I realized— this wasn't just about fixing the past. It was about finally letting ourselves feel everything we had buried deep inside. All the love, the anger, the sorrow.

We didn't need to say anything more. We just held on, as if holding on to each other could make the pain bearable.

This was not forgiveness yet. But it was a start.

And maybe... just maybe, it was enough for now.

As Lily turned to leave, her voice faltered, heavy with years of bottled emotions. "I don't believe you, Nile. You'll make me fall in love with you all over again... and then you'll leave." Her voice cracked, and her tears started to fall uncontrollably. "And I can't... I can't do it again. I don't know why I'm even crying. Maybe because I know that even if you leave, it'll still hurt... but nothing ever really changes for you, does it?"

She wiped her face in frustration, taking a step away. But before she could walk off, Uzair's soft, reassuring voice broke the silence. "Lily... please, don't walk away like this. You're making a mistake. I know it feels impossible right now, but trust me. Give him one chance." Uzair's voice was filled with warmth, conviction, and a kind of promise only a friend could give. "I swear... nothing will happen to you this time. I won't let it. I promise."

In the thick tension of the room, I glanced down and saw the flowers sitting on the table—simple, yet meaningful. Without hesitation, I grabbed them, knelt down on one knee in front of Lily, tears streaming down my face.

"Lily," I whispered, my voice breaking, "please... give me one chance. Just one. I know I can't undo the past... but I will fix everything. I swear, I'll do everything I can to make it right. Please."

Uzair gave Lily a small nod, his expression gentle yet firm, silently telling her that this was the moment to choose—to let go of the pain or carry it forever.

Lily looked down at me, her eyes filled with tears, her walls crumbling bit by bit. I could see the war inside her—years of hurt and betrayal fighting with the love she still carried deep in her heart. Her lips trembled, and her hands shook as she reached out to wipe the tears from my cheek.

And in that moment, with a soft, trembling breath, she whispered the word I had been desperate to hear: "Yes."

The word was quiet, but it felt like a roar in my soul, like the first ray of sunlight after endless nights of darkness. It was hope, redemption, and forgiveness all at once.

The weight that had suffocated me for years lifted, and suddenly, the future that once seemed impossible felt bright and within reach. I rose from my knees, pulling Lily into my arms, holding her close as we both cried—tears of relief, of love, and of a second chance.

"I'll fix everything, Lily," I whispered into her hair, my heart pounding against hers. "I swear, I'll make it all right. We were both broken once, but together… we'll heal. I promise you."

Lily held me tighter, as if holding on to this moment with everything she had. "Just don't leave me again, Nile," she whispered, her voice fragile and full of vulnerability.

"Never," I whispered back, pressing my forehead against hers. "Not ever again."

And in that embrace, for the first time in years, it felt like both of us were finally free—free from the pain, the regrets, and the past. Together, we had found the courage to step out of the darkness and into the light, ready to heal and build a future that was ours. Forever.

CHAPTER FOURTEEN

We sat at the dining table, the three of us, sharing love, laughter, and a sense of peace that felt new but comforting. Lily smiled warmly, her eyes soft as she said, "Hey, this dinner is *really* tasty, Nile."

Before I could respond, Uzair leaned back dramatically, patting his stomach with exaggerated satisfaction. "Mmm, yes! A culinary masterpiece by Chef Nile! You've finally done it—achieved the impossible! You made food I didn't want to drown in ketchup." He winked, and we all laughed.

I rolled my eyes. "You literally put ketchup on biryani last week, Uzair."

"That was a *creative touch*, my friend," Uzair said with a grin. "Gordon Ramsay would have cried tears of inspiration."

Lily giggled, and it felt like music—like a sound I'd been waiting to hear for years.

Uzair clapped his hands together suddenly, his face lighting up with excitement. "Alright, lovebirds, listen up! We've got three days left in London. Once we're back home, *operation wedding* is on. I'll fix the marriage date myself if I have to. I've been waiting to see you two finally come to your senses, and I'm *not* missing this chance!"

Lily shook her head, laughing softly. "I think the darkness might actually end now," she said, a hint of relief in her voice. Then her expression grew a little more serious. "Uzair... do you think I should reach out to my mom?"

Uzair's playful demeanor softened immediately. "Of course. Why wouldn't you?"

Lily sighed, looking down at her hands. "After you left, Nile... everything just fell apart. My dad left too. Mom wasn't in a good place, and I—I left as well. I was too broken to face her, so I just sent her money every month, hoping it would be enough."

Hearing that, I reached out and held her hand gently. "Lily... why are you working here, though? Why didn't you go back?"

Her voice was quiet, full of old wounds. "Because I didn't know how to. I felt so lost, and I was afraid she'd find out where I was and see the mess I'd become. I thought it was better this way... to disappear."

I squeezed her hand tightly. "I promise, Lily—I'll fix everything. We'll fix it together."

Just as the moment grew heavy, Uzair broke in with his classic comic timing, grinning mischievously. "Oh, great. Fixing things, huh? So... does that mean *you'll* finally learn to fix a flat tire, or is that still my department?"

I shot him a playful glare. "Hey, I'll fix life, Uzair—not *tires*."

Uzair put a hand on his heart, pretending to be hurt. "You know what, Nile? I never thought you'd betray me like this.

Here I was, dreaming that one day you'd call me the 'Mechanic Messiah.' But noooo—'fix life, not tires,' you said!"

Lily burst out laughing, and I couldn't help but join her. Seeing her laugh like that made every hardship worth it.

"Okay, okay," Uzair said, throwing his hands up. "I'll let it slide— for now. But, Nile, if you're fixing things... start by making sure you never let go of this one." He pointed to Lily with a grin.

I looked at her, my heart full. "Never," I said softly, and she smiled back, her hand still in mine.

And in that moment, it felt like the pieces of our lives were finally falling into place, with laughter, love, and a future we could now begin to rebuild—together.

Uzair chuckled, shaking his head. "Oh, come on, Nile! You can't just *wink* your way out of traditional rules! This isn't a rom-com; we can't just throw caution to the wind and break all the rules because you've got some newfound 'love' in your life!"

I raised an eyebrow and leaned in closer to Lily. "Well, I think tradition should be flexible, especially if you *really* care about someone." I winked at her again, my playful tone making her smile.

"Nice try, Casanova," Uzair said, crossing his arms and leaning back with a smirk. "But if I let you guys sleep in the same room, I'll have to explain to my mom why you're not wearing matching pajamas at the wedding!"

Lily burst out laughing, and I joined in, shaking my head. "Matching pajamas? Who wears those?"

Uzair leaned in with mock seriousness. "Oh, come on! You haven't lived until you've had a couple's pajama party! It's a rite of passage!"

I pretended to consider this. "Hmm, maybe that'll be our first *official* date. Dinner followed by a romantic pajama party! Very classy."

"Right, and you can share your favorite bedtime stories," Uzair added, his eyes sparkling with mischief. "I can just see it now: 'Once upon a time, in a land where Nile thought he could bypass tradition…'"

I laughed, shaking my head. "Don't you have some *actual* work to do, like organizing my wedding instead of critiquing my love life?"

"Touché!" Uzair replied, raising his hands in defeat. "But seriously, guys, keep it PG until the big day. We're trying to keep our *family-friendly* image here!"

"Yeah, yeah," I said, rolling my eyes but unable to hide my smile. "You're just jealous that you're not the star of this romantic saga!"

"Jealous? Please! I'm the proud producer behind this master-piece. Just remember, I get all the royalties when this love story hits the big screen!"

We all burst into laughter, the tension easing into a comfortable camaraderie. In that moment, surrounded by humour and warmth, it felt like the future was bright—full of love, friendship, and yes, maybe even matching pyjamas.

The sun filtered through the curtains, casting a warm glow in the room as I stretched and rubbed the sleep from my eyes. I was surprised to find Lily sitting beside me, a steaming cup of coffee in hand.

"Good morning, sleepyhead!" she said, a playful smile dancing on her lips.

"I really never thought this day would come again in my life," I replied, taking the coffee from her. The rich aroma filled the air, and I couldn't help but smile back.

Lily's expression softened. "Nile, I want to talk to Mom. It's been twelve years since I last saw her."

"Of course!" I replied, pulling out my phone and setting up a video call. The moment her mother picked up, her face lit up with joy.

"Lily, my dear! Is that you?" her mother exclaimed, her voice thick with emotion. "Oh, Nile! Did you find her? Is she okay?"

I grinned, pulling Lily closer. "All good, Mother-in-law! She's right here!"

Lily's mom squealed with delight, and I could see the happiness radiating from her. "Oh, thank you! Thank you so much, Nile!"

Lily took the phone, and they began discussing everything—memories, updates on life, and future plans. I watched them, my heart swelling at the sight of their reunion.

Just then, Uzair barged into the room with his usual enthusiasm. "Alright, lovebirds! I think we need to do some shopping for the wedding. Time to hit the town!"

Lily and I exchanged excited glances. "Shopping?" I echoed, feeling a rush of adrenaline.

Uzair clapped his hands, grinning from ear to ear. "Yes! We're talking dresses, suits, and maybe even a cake tasting! You know, the essentials!"

As we ventured out, the day turned into a delightful whirlwind. We started at a bridal shop, where Lily tried on dresses, twirling in front of the mirror. "What do you think?" she asked, her face alight with excitement as she slipped into a stunning gown. "Wow, you look like a princess!" I exclaimed, my eyes widening.

"More like a queen!" Uzair chimed in. "But let's not forget about the fitting for the groom. We can't have Nile overshadowing Lily on the big day!"

"Oh, please! You know I'm the main event here," I joked, striking a pose. "Just call me the prince!"

Lily laughed, shaking her head. "More like the jester!"

After a morning of trying on dresses, we moved on to the cake shop. The moment we walked in, our senses were assaulted by the sweet aroma of baked goods.

"What do you think, Nile?" Uzair asked, gesturing at an extravagant multi-tiered cake. "Should we go for something traditional or wild?"

I chuckled, eyeing the rainbow sprinkles adorning a vibrant cake. "Why not both? A little chaos never hurt anyone!"

Lily smirked, raising an eyebrow. "That sounds like you're just trying to sneak some sugar for yourself."

"Guilty as charged!" I laughed, grabbing a slice of the wild cake to sample. "Mmm! This is amazing!"

As the day went on, we shared countless laughs, playful banter, and heartfelt moments. Every step of the way felt like a celebration—a joyful reunion filled with love, hope, and a promise of new beginnings.

By the time we returned home, my heart felt lighter, and I knew that together, we were ready to take on the world—one shopping trip at a time!

The sun poured through the kitchen window as I sat at the breakfast table, eagerly waiting for my coffee to kick in. Uzair was already digging into a mountain of pancakes, while Lily floated in and out of the kitchen, preparing for her day.

"Hey, what's on the agenda today?" I asked, flipping through a magazine absentmindedly.

Lily looked up, a playful glint in her eyes. "I'm having a party with my friends today. Lots of catching up to do!"

"Oh, great!" I exclaimed, feigning despair. "I have to spend a whole day without you? How will I ever survive?"

Uzair, ever the comedian, chimed in, "You could always write a ballad about your love life! 'Oh, woe is me, left alone with pancakes!'" He dramatically placed a hand on his forehead, pretending to swoon.

"Ha ha, very funny," I shot back, rolling my eyes but unable to suppress a grin. "Maybe I should just start a support group for the 'Neglected Boyfriend Club.'"

"Count me in!" Uzair replied, raising his fork like a sword. "We can meet every Thursday at 7, right after I finish my pancakes."

Lily laughed, shaking her head as she finished packing her bag. "You two are ridiculous. Just remember to take care of yourselves while I'm gone! No burning down the apartment!"

As she headed toward the door, I felt a sudden rush of disappointment. I stood up and walked over to her. "Hey, wait a minute! No goodbye hug?"

She turned, her expression softening. "Of course!" With that, she stepped forward, wrapping her arms around me. I held her tightly, feeling the warmth of her embrace seep into my skin.

"Have fun," I whispered into her hair, not wanting to let go.

"I will!" she replied, pulling back slightly to look into my eyes. "And don't forget, I'll be back before you know it!"

With a playful grin, she slipped out the door, leaving me standing there with a mixture of joy and longing. I watched her walk away, already missing her presence, but I also felt a sense of excitement for her.

"See?" Uzair said, stuffing another piece of pancake in his mouth. "You survived the farewell! Now it's time to celebrate your freedom!"

I chuckled, shaking my head. "Freedom? More like impending boredom."

He waved a fork in the air. "Not on my watch! We've got a whole day to fill! Let's plan some epic shenanigans!"

With that, our day of adventures began, filled with laughter and the promise of fun, even without Lily by my side.

After spending the day with Uzair and his endless shenanigans, the evening rolled in. We'd watched movies, played ridiculous games, and even tried cooking—let's just say Uzair almost set the kitchen on fire, but we survived. As night settled, I was sprawled out on the couch, half-asleep, when the front door clicked open.

Lily walked in with the brightest smile, and before I could even sit up, she rushed toward me and wrapped me in the tightest hug. Her arms locked around me like she didn't want to let go, and honestly, I didn't either.

"I missed you," she whispered, her voice warm against my shoulder. "You know some of my friends are coming soon for the wedding... I'm so excited, Nile!"

I grinned, my heart full at the sound of her happiness, but before I could respond, Uzair's voice boomed from the other side of the room.

"Hey, hey, hey! Lily, ease up! The poor guy's turning purple. If you squeeze him any tighter, I'll need to call for an ambulance!"

Lily laughed, loosening her grip slightly but not letting go entirely.

"You're just jealous, Uzair," I said, looking at him from over Lily's shoulder.

Uzair grinned wickedly. "Jealous? Please. I'm just saying, if you suffocate him now, who's going to say 'I do' at the wedding? Me?" He struck a ridiculous pose like he was ready to take my place at the altar.

Lily laughed so hard she buried her face into my chest, trying to stifle her giggles. I couldn't help but smile, holding her close as if the whole world was in perfect harmony right now.

"See what I have to deal with?" I teased her. "This guy's a constant threat to my dignity."

Uzair scoffed. "It's not *my* fault you two are a walking soap opera. Someone's gotta keep things entertaining."

Lily looked up at me with a playful sparkle in her eyes. "Well, at least he keeps us laughing."

"And you," I added, pressing a kiss on her forehead, "keep me sane."

She smiled, her cheeks glowing. In that moment, it felt like everything was exactly where it should be—her in my arms, Uzair cracking jokes in the background, and the future feeling a little less uncertain.

Uzair clapped his hands together, breaking the moment. "Alright, lovebirds. Enough romance for one night, or you'll give me a toothache. Who's up for late-night snacks?"

Lily giggled as we all moved toward the kitchen, the night filled with lighthearted banter, snacks, and the kind of laughter that made everything feel right.

The next day flew by with laughter and joy, as if time itself wanted to run away from us. We roamed the streets, visited random shops, and made silly memories with Uzair being his usual hilarious self— he even challenged a street performer to a dance-off (which he lost miserably, but we all laughed until our stomachs hurt).

As night settled in, we gathered for dinner around the table, the warmth of the moment wrapping us in a cocoon of peace. Uzair, as usual, was the first to break the silence with his typical straightforwardness.

"Alright, guys," he announced, pausing dramatically with his fork in mid-air. "We're leaving tomorrow. Flight's in the evening, so don't even think of sleeping in too late. Be ready. And yes, Nile—" he shot me a look, "I mean *you*. No escape plans this time."

I chuckled softly, but my heart felt heavy at the thought of leaving. I glanced over at Lily, and at the same moment, she looked at me. For a second, everything else faded—the clinking of cutlery, Uzair's playful banter, the buzz of the outside world.

Our eyes locked, and it was like we were having a conversation without saying a word. There was a mixture of love, hope, and maybe even a little fear in her gaze. *Are we ready for this?* her eyes seemed to ask. And mine responded with silent reassurance: *We'll be okay.*

Uzair, oblivious to our unspoken exchange, continued talking as if the world hadn't just shifted.

"Look at you two, staring at each other like some cheesy romance movie." He smirked. "Just promise me you won't cry at the airport tomorrow. I'm already emotionally unavailable."

Lily snorted, trying to hold back her laughter, while I shook my head at Uzair's antics.

"Seriously, man?" I muttered, but I couldn't help but smile.

After finishing dinner, the weight of the day and everything that lay ahead caught up with us. One by one, we drifted off to our rooms, the house falling into a peaceful silence.

Lily and I shared one last glance before heading to bed—like two souls silently promising to hold onto each other no matter what tomorrow would bring.

And with that, we slept, each of us lost in our own thoughts, knowing that tomorrow held more than just a flight home—it held a new beginning.

CHAPTER FIFTEEN

As we were about to settle in for the night, Lily's phone buzzed. I picked it up, seeing her mom's name flashing on the screen. I answered with a smile.

"Hello, Nile! I'm so excited for tomorrow!" her mother's voice sang through the phone, brimming with joy. "It's going to be a beautiful day, and I can't wait to see everything come together."

Her excitement was contagious, and I found myself grinning ear to ear. "We're excited too, Mom. We'll make sure it's perfect."

We talked for a bit—just small, happy conversations about the wedding and life ahead. When the call ended, I set the phone down and looked at Lily, who was already smiling softly at me.

Without a second thought, I pulled her into a tight embrace, wrapping her in my arms as if I could shield us both from time itself. I buried my face into her hair, inhaling the familiar scent that I never wanted to forget.

"I really don't want to leave you, Lily," I whispered against her, my voice filled with emotion I couldn't hold back. My heart ached at the thought of parting, even if it was only until tomorrow.

She held me just as tightly, her arms squeezing around me like she didn't want to let go either. "I don't want to leave you, either," she murmured.

I kissed her forehead gently, my lips lingering there for a moment, savoring the peace I found in her presence. "Tomorrow starts a new life for us," I whispered softly. "I promise it will be beautiful."

She smiled, her eyes shining with unspoken emotion, and in that moment, it felt like everything in the universe had aligned just for us. We held each other close, hearts beating in sync, before finally letting go, though neither of us truly wanted to.

"See you tomorrow," I whispered.

"See you tomorrow," she replied with a soft smile, and we bid each other goodnight—knowing that tomorrow wasn't just another day. It was the beginning of a new life, one we would face together.

I lay down in bed, feeling light, like every burden had been lifted.

For the first time in a long while, I was truly, deeply happy.

The morning sun peeked through the curtains, but Lily was still sound asleep, her face peaceful and serene. I smiled to myself, thinking how beautiful she looked even in her dreams. I was tempted to wake her, but Uzair walked in, already sipping his coffee.

"Hey man, everything's packed?" I asked.

"Yeah, all set. But don't wake her, bro," Uzair said with a playful grin. "She's probably exhausted. Let her sleep. We've got a couple of hours before we need to leave."

I hesitated for a moment, standing at the door, torn between waking her up and letting her rest. Uzair gave me a pat on the shoulder. "Relax, lover boy. She'll wake up soon. Come on, let's grab some fresh air."

I gave in with a smile. "Alright, alright. Let her sleep. But we'll come back soon." We both stepped outside, soaking in the crisp air, hearts light with excitement for tomorrow. The feeling of everything finally falling into place was surreal, and I couldn't help but feel grateful for how far we'd come.

We wandered around, aimlessly enjoying our last few hours in this city, imagining the life ahead. As time ticked by, we knew we had to return soon. Just as I pulled out my phone to check the time, it rang. It was Lily.

"Hey, sweetheart," I answered warmly. "Did you sleep well?"

Still groggy, she mumbled, "Where are you guys? I just woke up."

I smiled, picturing her rubbing her eyes, trying to shake off the sleep. "We didn't want to disturb you, love, so Uzair and I went out for a bit. Do you want us to come back?"

There was a pause on the other end, followed by her soft voice. "I need to finish some packing. You guys carry on—I'll see you soon."

"Okay," I replied gently. "We'll be there soon. I love you, sweetheart."

Her voice was soft, filled with warmth. "Love you too. See you soon."

As the call ended, I leaned back, staring at the sky, feeling content in a way I hadn't for years. Uzair nudged me with a smirk. "Man, you sound like a teenager in love."

I laughed. "I guess I am."

We spent the rest of the day in a state of excitement, mentally preparing ourselves for tomorrow. Everything we had been through—every tear, every mistake—had led us here. And now, tomorrow awaited, a new beginning we had fought so hard to reach.

As we drove back, the excitement buzzed between us. We talked about the future, about the wedding, about the life waiting for us. On the way, I spotted a little shop with fresh flowers—roses, lilies, and baby's breath woven into a delicate bouquet. I knew these were Lily's favorites. Without thinking twice, I pulled over, bought the flowers, and smiled to myself.

She'll love these, I thought.

When we reached the apartment and parked the car, everything felt perfect. But as soon as we stepped out, something felt off— people were hurrying around, panic in their eyes, shouting on their phones. A man nearby was frantically calling an ambulance. My heart froze.

"Uzair… something's wrong."

I pushed forward, moving faster, fear creeping up my spine. The crowd gathered near the building's entrance, people whispering and staring. My stomach twisted. *No. No. No. She's waiting for me upstairs. She's fine. She has to be fine.* I sprinted through the crowd, Uzair following close behind.

And then I saw it.

At the heart of the chaos, there she was—Lily—lying motionless on the cold pavement, her delicate frame stained with blood. Her beautiful hair was tangled, and her head was bleeding heavily, the deep crimson spreading fast.

It felt like the world shattered in an instant. My legs gave way beneath me, and I collapsed to the ground, the bouquet slipping from my trembling hands. *This isn't real. This can't be real.*

"Lily!" I gasped, crawling toward her, tears streaming uncontrollably down my face. I gripped her hand—it was cold. My heart felt like it was being ripped apart. "Please, Lily… open your eyes. Please! Don't leave me!" My voice cracked, choked by sobs.

Uzair knelt beside me, his voice strained but calm. "Nile, we have to get her to the hospital. Come on, brother. Stay with me."

"No! She can't… I can't lose her!" I wailed, clinging to her lifeless form. My vision blurred as tears poured relentlessly, my heart screaming with guilt, pain, and helplessness. I had just found her—*we were supposed to start over.* How could everything fall apart again?

Uzair grabbed me by the shoulders, his own eyes glistening. "Nile, we can't help her like this. Stay with me! We need to get her to the hospital—NOW!"

The ambulance arrived, and paramedics rushed to her side, lifting her onto a stretcher. I stumbled after them, unable to breathe, the flowers still crumpled in my hand. Uzair pulled me close, supporting me as my knees buckled again.

"She'll make it, Nile. She'll make it," Uzair whispered, but his voice betrayed the fear in his heart. I clung to those words like a lifeline, even though the darkness was closing in on me.

The ambulance ride to the hospital was a blur. I couldn't stop shaking, couldn't stop the endless tears that flowed. Uzair kept one arm around me, holding me together as I fell apart. I kept whispering her name like a prayer, over and over, hoping it would reach her somehow. *Don't leave me, Lily… please.*

At the hospital, the doctors rushed her into the emergency room. They shouted codes and instructions I couldn't understand as the doors of the operation theater swung shut in front of me, leaving me on the other side—helpless and broken.

I crumbled onto a bench, my head in my hands. It felt like my soul had been ripped out of my chest, and all I could do was sit there, drowning in my own tears. Uzair sat beside me, his hand on my back, gently rubbing circles.

"Cry, Nile," Uzair whispered, his own voice shaky. "Let it out, brother. It's okay. Just cry." And I did— like a child who had lost everything, because I had.

The minutes stretched into what felt like an eternity. Every tick of the clock felt like a knife twisting deeper into my chest. She was behind those doors, fighting for her life, and I could do nothing but wait. My head sank into my hands, and I whispered through my sobs, "I can't lose her, Uzair. Not now. Not again."

Uzair pulled me close and whispered, "She's strong, Nile. Just like you. She's going to fight, and you're going to fight with her.

You're not alone in this."

But as I sat there, shivering and broken, I couldn't shake the gnawing fear in my heart: *What if I never get to tell her I love her one last time?

The door to the operation theater creaked open, and I jumped to my feet. My heart raced with hope and fear, as if every breath I took was keeping her alive. The doctor stepped out, her expression heavy with sorrow. I knew before she even spoke—*but I wasn't ready for it.*

"Was she with you?" the doctor asked softly, her voice almost hesitant.

"Yes," I whispered, my voice breaking, hoping against hope that the next words wouldn't confirm my worst nightmare.

She placed her hand gently on my shoulder, her eyes full of regret. "Life... life is unpredictable. We tried everything we could. But she..." The words came slower, each one a dagger to my heart. "She gave up. I'm sorry... she's gone."

My knees buckled, and I crumpled to the floor as if the ground beneath me had disappeared. *Gone?* No, that couldn't be. She promised. We promised each other. This wasn't how it was supposed end.

"She... left me?" I whispered, staring blankly at the floor, the weight of her absence crushing me. "We were supposed to start over... We were supposed to get married..." My voice cracked as I looked up at the doctor in disbelief. "No, she can't... she can't just leave."

Before anyone could stop me, I stumbled toward the ward, tears blurring my vision, my heart screaming with desperation. Uzair's voice echoed behind me, calling my name, but I couldn't hear him. I couldn't think.

I burst into the room and saw her—Lily—lying so still, so peaceful, as if she were only asleep. Her beautiful face looked exactly the same, untouched by pain, as if she was waiting for me to wake her. For a moment, it felt like time had stopped.

"No..." I whispered, dropping to my knees beside her. I reached for her hand, wrapping it in mine. It was cold. Too cold.

"Lily... come on, sweetheart. This isn't funny." My voice shook, tears spilling down my cheeks as I leaned closer. "You know we're getting married tomorrow, right? We missed the flight, but... no worries. We'll catch the next one. Just wake up, please. I'll fix everything. I swear I'll make things right."

I pulled her into my arms, hugging her tightly, rocking her gently as if my warmth could bring her back. "Please, Lily... don't leave me alone. I can't do this without you. I was lost without you once—I can't do it again. Please... just wake up." My sobs came uncontrollably now, my words tangled in desperation.

Uzair stood in the doorway, his eyes red and swollen, tears running down his face. He slowly stepped closer, his voice cracking as he whispered, "Nile... brother... she's gone."

"No!" I shouted, clutching Lily tighter. "She's not gone. She can't be! Uzair, tell her to wake up! She always listens to you!"

Uzair knelt beside me, placing a hand on my back, his own tears falling freely now. "I wish I could, brother... I wish I could." His voice was thick with grief, and I could feel his hand trembling.

I buried my face in her hair, inhaling her scent one last time, as if I could capture her essence and hold it within me forever. "Lily... I love you. I always loved you. I was just too stupid to say it sooner... Please don't leave me."

But there was no response. Just silence—heavy, crushing silence that wrapped around me like a noose, suffocating every ounce of hope I had left.

Uzair sat beside me, his arm around my shoulder as I broke down completely. We stayed there, two broken souls mourning the loss of the woman we both adored—one as a brother, the other as a lover.

The weight of the moment was unbearable. I kissed her forehead, my tears falling onto her skin, wishing I could trade places with her, wishing I could take back every mistake, every moment I hurt her.

"You were supposed to stay, Lily," I whispered one last time. "We were supposed to have a life together... Why did you leave me?"

Uzair pulled me closer, his own tears mixing with mine as we sat there, shattered and lost, holding on to the last remnants of the woman who had meant everything. The world outside kept moving, but inside that room, time stood still—nothing would ever be the same again.

They gave us permission to take her home. I lifted her gently, cradling her lifeless body in my arms, my hands trembling with every movement. She was so light, as if her soul had already drifted far beyond my reach. I kept whispering as I held her close, my voice breaking into pieces, "Lily, I love you... I love you, my bride... My Lily..." Each step I took felt heavier than the last, dragging me deeper into a place of endless pain.

Uzair walked beside me, silent, his head lowered, trying to stay strong, but I knew he was barely holding himself together. Every step toward home tore at my heart, each breath growing sharper, as if the air itself was rejecting my existence without her.

We reached her mother's house, and the second her mother saw us, she collapsed with a gut-wrenching scream that shattered the silence.

"No! Not my baby! Not my Lily!" she wailed, falling to her knees, pounding the ground as if she could tear apart the universe and bring her daughter back. Her sobs were unbearable—like the sound of a heart tearing itself apart.

I knelt beside her, still holding Lily in my arms, my own tears streaming endlessly down my face. Her mother ran her hands over Lily's cold cheeks, her hair, her lips, as if touching her would somehow change this nightmare. "Lily, my love... why did you leave me too? Why?"

Everyone around us was crying, but their sounds blurred into a distant hum. The world no longer made sense—just a swirling mess of grief, regrets, and broken promises.

I carried her toward the burial site. Every step was agonizing, the weight of her absence pressing down on me like stones tied to my soul. "I love you, Lily... I'll keep saying it until you hear me... I love you, my bride... please wake up. Please," I whispered, brushing a strand of hair from her pale face.

We reached the grave—an open, empty hole, dark and waiting, as if it had been expecting her. They told me to lay her down. My hands shook violently, and I couldn't let go. I kissed her forehead one last time, holding her close for a moment longer than they wanted.

"Goodbye, my love…" I whispered against her cold lips. "You promised me forever…" My words dissolved into sobs as I placed her gently into the earth.

Her mother clung to me, her cries a painful echo of my own heartbreak. "My baby! No, don't take her! Please don't take her from me!" But they gently pulled her back as the first shovels of dirt hit the coffin.

The sound of the sand hitting the wooden surface felt like nails being driven into my heart. With every handful of dirt, the world grew darker. I watched her disappear beneath the earth, inch by inch, my heart splintering with each fall of the soil.

"No… no, no…" I whispered, my knees giving out beneath me. I collapsed at the edge of the grave, grabbing fistfuls of dirt in my hands as if I could pull her back. "Please… no! Not like this! Not my Lily! She's supposed to be with me—she's supposed to be my wife!"

Uzair held me tightly, trying to keep me grounded, but I was breaking beyond repair. I screamed her name into the night, hoping somehow it would reach her. But all I got in return was silence.

And then, it was over. The grave was filled, the last piece of her hidden away from me. I knelt there, my fingers digging into the dirt above her, pressing my forehead to the earth as if I could feel her heartbeat beneath it.

The night was quiet, but the quiet wasn't peace—it was emptiness. The world around me blurred as my tears soaked the soil beneath me.

Uzair placed a hand on my shoulder, his voice soft, breaking. "Come on, Nile… It's done."

But I didn't move. I stayed there, gripping the dirt, pressing myself against the grave as if I could become one with it. "I'll stay, Uzair… I'll stay with her… I can't leave her alone again."

The sky above us was dark, without stars, and the cold wind whispered through the trees like a cruel reminder that life would go on without her. But mine wouldn't—not the way I'd imagined.

I traced her name on the small marker with trembling fingers. "I love you, Lily. Always. Forever. Just… wait for me there, okay?"

And then, for the first time since she left, the world felt truly silent.

The night was heavy, thick with silence, as I sat alone by Lily's grave. The cold earth beneath me was a cruel reminder of the reality I refused to accept. My fingers traced over the fresh soil, trembling as if somehow I could feel her heartbeat through it. Every moment I spent with her—every laugh, every touch, every promise—weighed down on me, dragging me deeper into the darkness.

I whispered softly, "I love you, Lily… I always will. I'll carry you with me, forever."

Tears rolled freely down my face, mixing with the dirt on my hands, but I didn't care. It felt like the world had collapsed, leaving me stranded in a place where time and meaning no longer existed.

Then, I felt a familiar hand on my shoulder—Uzair. He knelt beside me, his presence solid and grounding, the only thing keeping me from unraveling completely.

For a while, we sat in silence, the night wrapping around us. The stars above blinked faintly, distant and indifferent to the pain that gripped my soul. Uzair's voice finally broke through the stillness, low and deliberate.

"Nile…" he whispered, "this wasn't an accident."

The words hit me like a blow to the chest. I turned to him, confusion swirling in my mind. "What are you saying?"

Uzair didn't meet my gaze immediately, as if speaking the words made them more real. "It wasn't an accident… It was murder."

Everything inside me froze. The world seemed to tilt, and for a moment, I couldn't breathe. Murder? No. No, it couldn't be. My mind refused to wrap around the idea, the truth too cruel to comprehend.

But as the weight of Uzair's words settled over me, the cold night seemed even darker, and the grief inside me twisted into something sharper, heavier.

I stared at the grave, my heart a shattered mess, my mind lost between disbelief and anguish. The one person I thought I could hold onto was gone, and now—now there was something more.

Something I couldn't understand.

The wind whispered through the night, carrying with it the heavy promise of unanswered questions.

The breeze stirred the leaves, carrying away the soft whispers of the night. Somewhere in the distance, the city continued its life, unaware of the ache that swallowed me whole. I closed my eyes, holding onto the last memories of her touch, her smile, her laugh.

The only thing left now was the silence—deep, heavy, and unrelenting. And in that silence, something stirred—a question, a suspicion, and a truth waiting in the darkness, just out of reach.

Epilogue

As Nile stood on that familiar hilltop, a wave of determination surged through him. While he had begun to embrace the light within, he knew that shadows still lurked in the corners of his life— unresolved issues that demanded his attention. There were those who had wronged him and the people he loved, and he could feel the weight of their actions pressing down on him.

With thoughts of revenge flickering in his mind, he realized that confronting the past was not just about seeking closure but also about reclaiming his power. He was ready to uncover the truth and confront those who had tried to dim his light. The journey ahead would not only test his strength but also reveal the true depths of his character.

As he stepped forward, Nile understood that the battle was not just against external forces but also against the darkness within. The future held challenges, and while he sought to heal and grow, he also knew he would have to face those who threatened the peace he had fought so hard to achieve. The stakes were high, and the path to justice was fraught with danger.

Nile's story was far from over, and the thrill of revenge intertwined with his quest for self-discovery promised to shape the next chapter in ways he could not yet imagine.